# DARK INTENTIONS

Vampire Matchmaking Agency

Book 1

Dark Intentions:
Edited by: Jennifer Miller
Book Formatting: Jennifer Eaton
Cover Designer: DeliciousNightsDesigns.com

*For my siblings, who always have my back.*

PROLOGUE

*Three Years Ago...*

Leila nearly slid down her stool, not even attempting to stifle her giggles. "Girl, stop it. Please, I can't take much more."

It was the playful, good type of laughter. Not the kind that meant they'd bare fangs and filet one another, a hallmark of vampire interactions.

"I told you already..."

Plates clinked together and blended with instrumental hip-hop set to low, accented with the buzzing voices of nearby guests. It was another filled-to-the-rafters Saturday night at Melody, one of Leila's clubs located in Harmony Park near downtown Detroit.

"You did," Leila said, taking a sip of a drink called a Jack Handle, presumably due to the aftereffects on humans who were unlucky enough to order too many. A bout of laughter overtook her once more, and she held onto the counter while struggling to breathe. Even if it took a few moments to regain her composure, Leila continued, undeterred by Farrah's sour expression. "I just wanna hear it again... At least, show me his profile pic."

Farrah struggled to disguise her wince. "Why?" she stalled. After years of being Leila's companion, her maker's MO wasn't a secret. She would dismiss any emotional attachment to a human. Then she would ride Farrah even worse for her momentary lapse of judgment.

Sitting in the nouveau-chic environment against a backdrop of high-octane lacquer furnishings, LED lights, and gorgeous males, there was no way Leila would get why Farrah was upset over one excruciatingly ordinary human.

"Show me. Because if you don't, it means you knew he wasn't worth your time in the first place."

Reluctantly... begrudgingly, Farrah pulled her iPhone from inside her denim jacket and opened the dating profile on sendmeamatch.com's app. Once the frustration over his rejection was all gone, he didn't look as intriguing as he had before. Now, sitting there being forced to show him somehow illuminated every bit of his fallibility. "Here."

Leila took the phone and held it out a full arm's length from her as if she expected it to stink of the human. "Wow. Man," she whispered, surveying his girth, his thinning hair, his underperforming jawline. "To think you would have brought this mess home. And that sweater," she said, twisting the phone to the side as if to get a better perspective. "So tight. Is that what humans call onesies?"

"He's not so bad." Farrah took the phone out of Leila's casket-shaped nails, slipped it back into her pocket, and returned to her drink. "Of course, it wasn't supposed to be for-*ever*. It's just something to do. Something I needed to do. He may not have been hot, like at all, but he was someone I thought would see past the superficial."

She lied. The real truth was, if she dated this mediocre human, she would at least be able to feel better about herself. Covering for her deficits up close and in person was a lot harder than holding her mask in place around the *others*. She hadn't even been doing a wonderful job of it. Farrah knew they could smell her weaknesses. And that was something she hadn't wanted to deal with in her bedroom, and in affairs of the heart.

It would have been easier if there weren't so many prejudices within the supernatural races. Not to mention how scattered all the immortals were. Most of that was due to the prehistoric beliefs of the Order of Immortals. They didn't allow any new inductions into covens, or any pack, horde, or clan like in the old days. Though these rules appeared arbitrary, the meaning was clear. There was to be no intermarrying, no building of factions, no crossing the invisible lines that separated the races.

Then there were the logistics of it all. Vampires suffered when blood-mated to other vampires. When mated, their powers, energy, and strength became shared resources. This was less of a problem centuries ago, when being separated from your mate was less likely and traveling in packs was more common. This balance of power had enhanced the dominance of the clan. One would think evolution would have done away with such a thing. But it hadn't. Without a unified show of force, having half your power shared with some fuck boy could be problematic.

That was the thing. Vampires should have been anxious to mate, but without the barbaric needs of the old days, the draw of mating was gone. It was almost as if love were forbidden, even if it wasn't.

Then there was Farrah herself. Where most vampires did a wonderful job of living up to the make-believe lore, she was not one of them. She struggled with turning off the part of her that was human, while most developed a thicker skin from the moment they were turned. They didn't bother with the constraints of human culture, like marriage and monogamy.

But Farrah knew there was a mate out there for her. There was actually some internal drive that commanded her to find *him*. The one. Whoever the hell that was. As if she were cursed. And, just in the way of most curses, there were no directions that came with the sonofabitch. Only the will and drive. Sure, she had the will, but the drive, not so much. She actually felt as if she were being driven insane. It was like a venomous bite slinking its way through her body.

"I can't imagine what you see in humans. Even with sex, they are no real match for us"—Leila childishly made a hole with one hand and stuck her finger through it—"on their best day. Clearly, not this dude. But some of them might come close. I can even name a few. Apparently, Hollywood is where you need to find them." She straightened herself on the stool. "Even if you happen to find one that contradicts all those things, their lifespan is too short... a human will never satisfy you like another vampire. This is easy math that doesn't add up. I know you're smarter than that, girl."

Farrah knew her dearest friend and maker was probably right, as usual. Okay, she was mostly right. She just wasn't so sure being with a vampire would end her troubles. Hell, it hadn't so far. Whatever it was—activism or preservation—with the vampire race in the minority, exploring other options probably wasn't a bad idea. Still, a part of her knew humans were not *it*. And most vampires made her slightly ill at the thought.

"All valid points, Leila. I'm just wondering what else is out there. And the last time I dated a vampire, he was an absolute asshole—like for real. He always practically drained our host before offering me a vein. And he would go to bed without worrying about what I'd do to protect myself for the day. Hell, if I were being crisped in the sun, it wouldn't have made a bit of difference to him. You remember that, right?" Farrah huffed, running her fingers through errant tufts of hair to smooth the wild curls from her face. She'd forgotten her clip, and try as she might, she never achieved the Beyoncé look. She ventured more in the neighborhood of Glenn Close in *Fatal Attraction*, right around the time she was being stabbed in the shower. Or perhaps when she was on that roller coaster with the kid. But what did it matter? Anyone who sat next to Leila would pale in comparison.

"Yes, but at least he understood your plight and where you were coming from. Try getting a human to understand why you're not able to luxuriate on the beach all summer. And to make matters worse, your last fang bang was two decades ago. You might have been too young for him then. I've got an idea, though..." Leila tapped her fingernails on the black marble bar top.

Farrah took another drink, rolled her eyes, and motioned to the bartender to bring them another round. Mike the bartender was interesting and exactly the type of human Leila would approve of for one of their "fun" nights. His joggers were slung low around his waist, and Farrah was willing to bet the last pint of blood in the world he wasn't wearing BVDs since his manhood jostled freely as he sauntered—swaggered—up to the bar. He worked at Melody on Saturday nights. And while Farrah had never made a move on him, human that he was, they'd connected. Maybe it was purely due to him making the best drinks in the world. And that was on some spiritual shit.

Despite all that, she didn't want to sleep with him and mess up her nightly visits to the only vampire bar in her neighborhood. Some risks just weren't worth it.

Turning back to Leila, Farrah leveled her with her best skeptical glance. "What's your idea this time? I end up doing the craziest shit with you. Like when we went to meet the Australians."

Leila choked on her drink, laughing, her aquamarine eyes lit with amusement. "That was three decades ago, and as I recall, I had to kick the one you hooked up with out of our flat in London."

"Momentary lapse in judgement or whatever. What's this idea of yours?" With a wave of her hand, Farrah hurried the big idea along, and more importantly, away from the touchy, ancient hookup discussion.

Leila took a sip of her drink first, indicating it was definitely going to be a whopper. "So, there's a coven of sorts in northern Canada that has nothing but men who've taken a vow of—"

"Hell no."

"You didn't even let me get it out."

"I don't want to. Why would I want to travel to northern Canada to try to get someone to change their mind about sex or dating or being a vampire, for all I know, when they've taken a vow against whatev—"

"Because it's fun."

"It's not fun. In fact, that's the last thing I would call it. It's trying to alter someone's line of thinking when they've made a firm decision about who they want to be. They moved to northern Canada... I'm assuming you aren't talking Toronto?"

"I need to help you brush up on your geography."

Ignoring the jab was probably Farrah's best option. "I just think... Scratch that, I *know* there are other vampires out there who are like me. Maybe they want to date a non-vampire, too. Okay, so maybe not human. What about weres and shifters? How about dreamwalkers? Leprechauns... What if we're all just too chicken shit to try for love outside of what we know?"

"Or maybe we're all too smart for it. Look where it gets most humans. They end up splitting up property, hating one another, and divvying up kids like they're assets." Leila shook her head.

"Maybe you're right, but maybe not. I just believe somehow... Leprechauns need love, too. There's gotta be someone who has a tall, dark, and green fetish among us. I think it should be okay to date and be with whom—whatever you want to be with."

That's when Leila fully turned to face Farrah, her stilettos hooked into the metal footrest and hands on her hips. "Farrah, I think your idealism is admirable... for a human. Which you aren't."

There were days when Farrah thought her friend had selective hearing. "And look at where that kind of thinking has gotten me. We can do something about it." Turning the frosty glass between her fingers, she spared Leila a glance once again. Determination speared Farrah in the gut as she met Leila's skeptical glare head-on.

"We?"

"You, me, the dark web. We're going to do some shit. And this isn't out of the blue, either. I found a personality profile to guide matches. It's human-psychology based, but how different could it be?"

"A lot. It's probably like a whole lot different." Leila's voice squeaked as she sipped her drink.

"So. So what? It's worth a try. Because right now, all we have are devices humans use. Like you said, they can't take our needs into consideration."

Leila's lids suddenly lowered, eyes near slits as she leaned in closer. "And you don't think the Order will have some concern over all this comingling?" Her brows nearly touched with concern.

"Now who's talking like a human?"

"I'm just trying to get you to see this is a terrible idea. You'll end up with your heart in a sling. Mark my words."

"You think that. You haven't even tried it. Ever."

"You don't know what I've tried," Leila snapped. For a moment, she stared down at the bar at unmoving hands. It took her a moment before she started again. "The paramount issue is, it's best if we stick to our own kind."

"Love is love, Leila." Farrah took another sip of her drink, trying hard not to let on that she'd stolen that from a human protest sign on a nightly news program.

"You just wanna get laid," Leila retorted, her snort as condescending as it was audible.

The noise in the bar around them grew louder, a sure sign it would be a night filled with mayhem and rabble-rousing. Humans had always perked up around the weekends, Not much had changed since the eighties, when Farrah had been turned.

The lighting went from dim to near darkness, and the music growing louder marked the evening hour of eleven, a time when the connections between the patrons went from business and platonic to lusty and sexual.

"I would be remiss if I didn't acknowledge this one point in the argument. But think about it. We've only ever been with vampires. What if someone else out there can truly make us happy?"

"Speak for yourself, boo. I, for one, do not limit myself. I'm not closed-minded. I just don't want to end up on the Order's most wanted list."

Farrah looked at her friend. Her maker. She knew her expression to be one of concern. "Hmph... they must be bored these days." She hadn't seen the Order enforce any of the old accords lately. All they seemed to do was collect taxes. A supernatural IRS. Still, the rumors of what they'd done to people in the past were petrifying. The thought of being flayed sent a shiver up Farrah's spine but did nothing to deter her.

"They could be. It's plausible." Leila turned on her stool toward the bar and grabbed her cocktail, tipping the glass up and draining the last sip into her mouth.

"Fine, chick. Whatevs." Farrah picked up her fresh drink and sputtered. That was definitely stronger than the others. Back as a human on a night like tonight, she would have been on her way to being shitfaced. Undoubtedly, Mike was trying to get her there in the hopes of getting her to his place. That was all he wanted, like most males. She could see it in his eyes, not to mention the pheromones he was throwing off. Pheromones were like a beacon to vampires, with their heightened sense of smell.

Silence expanded between them for a few seconds. While she didn't know what was on Leila's mind, she was thinking of her plan—to open a matchmaking agency. But what would she call it? Before she could come up with a name, Mike's fine ass brought their third round of drinks. Farrah downed the second and moved on to the next. Alcohol was one of the few substances on earth that had similar effects on humans as it did vampires, although it took them a lot longer to get blitzed than it did the humans. Well, except Farrah, that was. Though she was much more resistant to alcohol than she had been as a human, she thought she got a little bit more intoxicated than others.

Before leaving, Mike flashed a kilowatt, fang-free smile. There were humans in the dining areas until after two a.m. each night so vamps had to maintain their best behavior until the blood donors were gone. No one wanted the Order breathing down their necks, so most complied with the laws. "Thank you, honey. You are just as sweet as pie," she said to Mike, adding a gentle nod of her head.

"You're welcome." He allowed his fingers to linger on her hands a few seconds longer than necessary when he passed the drink to her.

No doubt about it, he was as hot as fish grease, but still. Hands off. Leila liked him. She'd probably never claim him, but something in her eyes told her secrets. She did like him, and he was sure as hell hot enough. Even if she wouldn't admit it.

"So," Leila said, "you ready to eat? Are we hunting tonight or just going out back for one of the feeders?"

"Ugggh," Farrah said, not reining in her level of dissatisfaction even a little bit. "I hate the feeders. Their veins are always unstable. There's nothing like feeding from an untapped vein. You know what I mean? I'd rather get a bag from the fridge and turn on the Hallmark Channel..."

"Lame, but yeah, I do. So... it sounds like we're hunting.... How about we go see make-a-match dude?"

"It's sendmeamatch."

"Whatevs. Matchmaker, matchmaker, send me whoever the hell, let's go over there."

"No. And fucking no. He doesn't deserve the ecstasy of a bite." Farrah scrunched her face and made a gagging sound to punctuate her disdain.

"What you should have done was charmed that ass last night. Sure, he wouldn't have remembered a damn thing this morning, but at least you wouldn't have gotten dumped."

"I can't even with you. I thought we were going to date for a while. Isn't it wrong to feed off him with friends? I don't want the karma behind something like that," Farrah said on a sigh.

"He left you sitting alone in a restaurant while he picked up some chick and left with her. Mind you, leaving you with the check."

"I know, but we weren't exactly hitting it off in person. I'm kind of glad it didn't go any further. I would have had to wipe his memory and all that. A few orgasms, *if* I was lucky, isn't worth that."

"You aren't sleeping with the right people, my friend. C'mon... let's go. His veins are untapped... he'll be as fresh as a daisy or some other human bullcrap." Leila was smiling again. By now, Farrah should have known a smile like that was not the blood bag and Hallmark kind.

"Girl, you are thirsty as hell. I'm not going to show up at this dude's house. With a friend in tow. Random as fuck. Do you know what he'll think?" Farrah wondered why she should even care what he thought. They would wipe his memory clean of any doubt, so why would it matter? Because he'd wounded her. She didn't want to give him even a moment of satisfaction, whether he remembered or not. "No. I don't give a care if he won't remember it. It's too good for him."

"All right. So, we go in through the window on some old Bram Stoker shit?"

"No. Really, I'll pass on that," Farrah started, with a shake of her head knowing full well giving in was only seconds behind that no. "Yes, fine. We'll get over there. I'll knock on the door all like, *yes, I brought my friend by, and we just want to talk to you for a second.* Okay?" Fluttering her lashes, Farrah pouted and licked her lips, feigning hunger.

Leila ran elegant fingers over her chin. "Yes and yes."

"So, this is technically not hunting, though..."

"But it'll feel like it..."

She rolled her eyes. "C'mon. Let's go. He lives all the way downriver."

"Driving or flying?"

"Driving. I have my Benz outside," Farrah said.

"I like that car."

"Yeah, me too. Pay the man. It's almost midnight. I'm fucking starving. I was so distraught, I didn't eat anything at sundown."

"Not even a snack? What is wrong with you? You could have jumped one of these humans. Don't do that, sis. Do better."

"I don't need your judgment right now. Let's just go." With a pop on Leila's shoulder, Farrah slid from the stool and waited.

Leila smiled in victory as she lay cash on the counter for Mike. Despite owning the joint, she took exceptionally good care of her waitstaff. "All right, let's go make this asshole's night. It'll be the best time he's ever forgotten."

Farrah didn't bother commenting. Instead, she led to way to her car, a black Benz S-Class. It was probably the only fashionable thing she owed.

As she slid into the car and plugged Stan's address into her phone, the perfect name for her new business popped into her mind. Vampire Matchmaking Agency. Sure, it was simple, but weren't the best things in life?

CHAPTER ONE

Sure, Farrah had found hundreds of mates for others in the three years since VMA had been open, but what about her own love life? Looking out over the life she'd created, it was nothing like what she'd envisioned over the years. But, at least she was doing something to help out the community.

The entrance bell rang on the Vintage Modernism Authority, the antique furniture store serving as body double for Vampire Matchmaking Agency. The name was terrible, something Leila noted frequently, but the moniker served its purpose. There were two distinct phone lines. If humans happened to be in the store, at least Farrah would know which to safely answer. Fortunately, humans rarely came in since the pieces in the shop were a bit overpriced for the area. Win, win.

The patron, a well-dressed female, looked like a supermodel with her ice-blue tendrils flowing down her back and her hourglass figure. Her dark skin was smooth, unmarred. Overdone makeup masked delicate features. *Fae.* She was who humans believed to be woodland creatures who spread glitter from the Highlands to the Americas and granted gifts. In reality, fae were much more complicated and dangerous than that. Like most human knowledge of lore, human understanding of the fae was skewed.

From the looks of her, this wasn't just some ran-doh fairy. Nope. This was high fae. Normally, they cloaked themselves, but since she hadn't, she probably knew VMA would be a safe space. The interesting thing was, why on earth would someone like this, obvious royalty, need a matchmaker?

Instead of walking to the counter where Farrah waited, she stopped, clutching a small, iridescent purse with both hands. It was impossible to miss that her eyes and cheeks were dusted in the same brilliantly multifaceted hue as her handbag.

"Hi there." Farrah stepped from behind the counter, fighting the urge to wipe her hands on her jeans to keep from sullying the pristine creature before her. Extending her hand, she waited as the stunning, surely princess-if-not-queen glanced down and hesitated as if she didn't know whether to accept the gesture or not.

Finally, she grasped Farrah's hand and awkwardly smiled. "Hello there," she said, her voice wispy and light. "My name is Eire, of Clan Seelie. I probably should have called ahead, but I'm interested in your... services." Typical of what Farrah had heard of the fae, even her accent was over the top. Her demeanor, though... it almost seemed understated in comparison to the makeup, the jewelry. All of it was over the top, but not her person. This Eire seemed as if she were trying on someone else's body to see if it fit.

Sheesh, she smelled like cotton candy and happiness.

"Don't be silly. Our doors are always open... well, except when they're closed during the day." *Wow, Farrah, lame much?* Releasing the hand she'd been holding for too long, she motioned over to the table in the sitting area she reserved for clients. A seventeenth-century French, Golden-Age table, chaise, and settee, along with some ornate, high-back chairs of unknown origin she'd procured from Leila's storage, filled the space. All she knew was they looked rich and elegant. "Um, would you like to have a seat, and we can discuss what you're looking for in a mate?"

"Yes, thank you." Eire walked over to the chair, and no matter how nice the area was, she made it look a million times better. Her white pants suit was wide-legged, the voluminous fabric spilling over the seat like the most elegant of ballgowns.

Farrah's original thought of Eire echoed in her mind once again. *There is no way this chick needs help finding a mate...* Following her, Farrah took the seat opposite Eire and opened the stationary laptop to start a new profile. "You're welcome. So, we can start with you telling me a bit about yourself." Once the profile was open to the notes tab, Farrah sat forward in her chair and offered a smile. One thing she knew, no matter who the client was, getting them to open up about who they were was the hardest part of the whole transaction.

"I am the daughter of Tarik, King of Clan Seelie. He has dominion and is the laird for all fae creatures. Even the unseelie, though they rebuke him."

Farrah tried hard to suppress her joy at being right. It wasn't that difficult, considering a part of her was nervous about whether this fae was really there just to spy on her and VMA. "Um... are you a member of the Order, Eire?"

Shit, she should have asked her that before. Given everything she knew about the fae, they were her least likely clients.

"Oh no. I am not. My father holds the fae seat. I will be, though, if anything were to happen to him." The only thing that could happen to him would be a lead stake in his heart, which was about as likely as a pig flying. "I do not follow the Order's antiquated philosophies."

If there was one thing Farrah was good at, it was reading folks. "I see. So, for the most part, your shit with following rules is the primary reason you're struggling to find a mate? I can imagine the implications of all that are challenging." She almost wanted to offer her hand in support, but despite how nice Eire was, she didn't seem like a hugger.

Eire sat back in her seat, allowing her pristine posture to droop, as if the winds were coming out of her sails a bit. "Yes, it's all so difficult to navigate. You see, it is tradition to marry a... a warrior who is chosen by your father." While Eire was staring directly at Farrah, her eyes seemed to travel miles away.

"And you don't want that?"

"I don't know whether I want to mate this male or not. All I know is it doesn't feel right... if I've never known another. What I mean to say is, I've never known another intimately. I mean, I'm still young. I'm only two hundred years old."

Eire was turning out to be as sweet as she was gorgeous and was a departure from most things Farrah thought she knew of their kind. "I understand. And I think we can help you with that. I can share some profiles of males with you tod—"

"I should add," Eire said, cutting Farrah off, "I would

like to limit my search to... what should I call them? Civilians?"

The request shocked Farrah. Wasn't everyone *civilians*? "Probably not civilians. Maybe just males, or females... You also don't have to worry about the Order. We don't service them here. In fact, we try hard to stay off their radar altogether." Farrah studied Eire's face to see if she had a tell. Farrah wished she could read minds, instead of just change them telepathically. The skill would have been useful in cases where she didn't know what to think. Eire's kind were supposed to be vapid killers, treacherous and cunning. She didn't appear to be any of those things.

"I guess um... I'm still figuring all that out. You see... the fae don't have to worry about such things in our race since we can be *whatever* we want for periods of time. Male or female."

Farrah's brows popped. That was definitely new info. Since Eire was VMA's first fae client, she added it to her mental filing system. *Date a fae...* "Okay, good to know. I should warn you, however, not all races have this ability on demand. Will that be a problem?" Sure, Eire should have known that, but she seemed like an innocent. Someone who hadn't ventured far from her realm.

"I think the question is, will that be a problem for them?"

Farrah thought on this for a moment. Could it be? Most supernaturals had hard limits set on humans, not sex. "How about we add *seeking gender-fluid mates* to your profile?"

"Yes?" Eire shifted and stared off for a moment as if considering the possibilities. "Yes, I think that will work. If gender-fluid is what I would be considered, then yes."

"I believe it would. So, you've told me a lot about what you need. Let's focus on what you want now, shall we?"

Eire nodded. For the first time, her eyes were wide with what appeared to be enthusiasm. She laid the shiny purse on the table and leaned forward. "Do you think I could meet someone quickly?"

Farrah wondered how someone so gorgeous could question whether she would meet someone quickly. Thankfully, pictures were locked down in the profiles until the client was matched, since the focus was on who the clients were and not what they looked like. Instead, they added photos of points of interest, hobbies, and favorite things to lend to their personalities. Otherwise, some of Farrah's more beguiling clients would have a bunch of "swipe rights" and not much substance. That wasn't VMA's mission. It'd worked so far. "Yes, I think you will meet someone. I've matched so many couples, I should attach a mating chapel."

They both laughed at that, and Eire began a list of her wildest fantasies, including vacations to remote parts of Earth and her deepest desires for love and life to complement and fulfill her.

Just as the convo was going well, the doorbell sounded out. Farrah glanced away from Eire to her newest guest. It was one of her clients, Violet. "Hey, Violet, I'll be with you in just a moment." Violet, unlike Eire, did have an appointment, so she felt the need to acknowledge her presence.

"Eire—" She returned her attention to the current conversation and stopped short. Now that was definitely different. She'd never had a client ghost her before, and even if she had, this instance would be extreme. Eire was gone. Simply slipped into the ether and faded away.

"Eire?" Farrah stood from the table and glanced around the room. No sign of her. Anywhere. "Right... well, Violet, I guess I'm ready for you now."

"Oh, okay. Who were you talking to when I came in?" Violet walked over, pulling her dyed silver hair back away from her face. She practically floated over and was everything Farrah wasn't as a vampire. She had come to VMA in search of something deeper than what was offered by the typical vampire nightlife.

"I was just..." Thinking back to the privacy that Eire had been concerned about, she stopped. "I was talking to myself. Just getting some things organized on my client profiles." She saved and closed Eire's profile, then smiled brightly up at Violet.

"No problem, sweetness." Violet had an overtly flirtatious way of speaking to everyone. "I have to tell you, my last date was kind of a bust. I mean, he was fine, but I'm not into his vibe. Can we modify my profile a little?"

"Sure." While Farrah was genuinely concerned about Violet's needs, where exactly in the fuck did Eire go? Was she still there, just hidden? Farrah didn't know all the powers the fae had, since they were largely elusive. Maybe she was just cloaked... "I just need to go get a notebook. I'll be right back." Farrah didn't wait for Violet's agreement.

Stepping away, she panned the room, glancing under tables as she passed them and trying to fathom where Eire could have possibly gone. By the time she got to the counter in the center of the room, she was utterly confused.

Moving behind the counter, she reached for her

"Stranger Things" notebook. As she grabbed it, a slip of white paper hit the floor. As she bent over to pick it up, a slow and deliberate script of iridescent ink formed before her eyes. *I'm sorry to leave so abruptly, but I cannot afford to be seen here. I'll be in touch...*

*Oh yeah, there's nothing strange about this at all.* Farrah folded the letter and placed it in her back pocket. She hadn't gotten Eire's number, so there was nothing else to do but wait for her to get in touch. She had heard the fae were unpredictable. At least that was one thing that already held true in Eire's case.

"Where the hell have you been?" While Anwar Tsedek knew he was being unreasonable, he was the one in dire straits. He didn't want a mate at all—much less one that had been chosen for him. As his homeland had shaken free of the ground and sunk into the sea, he had seen hundreds dive into the ruins to save their mates' lives. Of course, those were the days of lifelong relationships and well before Instagram. He'd seen the vampires born of Atlantean blood go from a vulnerable new race to vapid, dangerous savages. He'd seen, over the centuries, what he viewed as the ruin of civilization, several times over. The last thing he wanted to do was commit himself to a mate. But now he had to.

Thanks to an ancient agreement between his father and the Order, his life was about to be unavoidably and irreparably altered. He would have to be mated by the next grand assembly if Atlanteans were to remain constituents of the Order. It was a stupid agreement, one his father had supported since the witches who had cursed their race were still out there. He needed the protection and unity of the Order of Immortals. Otherwise, the Atlanteans would die off.

Since there was no way to break the accord, or to do so without bringing harm to House Tsedek, he needed a solid plan. Otherwise, his father, Constantine, would awaken to a world much different than the one he'd left.

Mael stepped inside the overly gilded office—one Anwar would have never chosen for himself, but he'd had no choice in the matter. As Anwar's personal *attaché*, Maelstrom should have been right by his side planning an escape, not gallivanting around the world.

"I've been trying to get you out of this mess," Mael said. "I would think you'd be happy I'm working so diligently on your behalf, my liege." The male, who still walked as if a glorious set of raven-colored wings were beset on his broad shoulders, stifled what looked to be a grin. The icy coolness in his accent was made harsh by the absence of his Enochian aura, stripped from him during his fall. "So, do you want to hear my idea, or are you resigned to sulking until you attempt plunging to your death out that window? I figure about halfway down, you'll remember you are an immortal."

Anwar shifted in the oversized chair, not in the mood for Mael's humor, and looked through the tempered glass into the night. The illuminated Detroit skyline muted the stars, even from his seat hundreds of feet above the beating heart of the city. "Go on. It had better be good. I cannot waste time on things that will not appease the Order. The lot of them are rabid over this notion of a mating."

"The Vampire Matchmaking Agency is the answer."

Anwar leaned forward, the leather seat creaking as he leveled a deathly glare on the closest being in the world to him. Mael, who seemed utterly and completely unbothered by the preposterous thing he'd just suggested, was taking a seat on the settee while going through great pains to gently rest his wool overcoat. "You want me to swipe left or right for a potential mate? How the hell would that be any better than mating Eire?"

The smack of wood sang out across the cavernous room. While Tarik had thrown the offer on the table, it wasn't as if the Order was forcing Anwar's hand. His proverbial hand was being forced by the ancient agreement. Each race had twelve months to fulfill the specific guidelines for remaining a represented group in the Order. It was specific, restrictive, and considering Anwar had squandered eleven months of his time, becoming dire.

"You're only pissed because you can't scream at this thing and make it go away." Maelstrom leaned back in the chair as if he'd won the prize, only serving to kick the hornet's nest that was Anwar's abject disdain for the Order even harder.

The Westborn suites atop the tallest building in Detroit, and every other thing afforded to Anwar and his family, had been courtesy of the Order. Therefore, not wanting to follow the rules set forth by the bastards seemed like true first-world problems.

"Is it unreasonable for me to want to pick my own mate, Mael?" While he hadn't intended for his voice to come out in a roar, he meant every single word of it. The truth was, while Anwar knew he had to pick someone, he didn't want to deal with a mate. There had never been an Atlantean who had truly loved another. He'd certainly seen love, but not in the way it was supposed to be. It was all a lie. Constantine had shown him that when Anwar's mother had died and Constantine had simply plucked another from the vine. It had been the same for all of the Atlanteans. As most of their population had sunk into what was now the Atlantic Ocean, it was a matter of Anwar choosing a tolerable mate and dealing with them for all eternity, or until they met their end. "This is not the Order's place. We've been held responsible for something my father agreed to hundreds of years ago. I was but a boy with no choices."

"I can see in all those years, you've managed to control your anger. What is the saying? There comes a time when a male must put down his childish things." Mael stood and picked imaginary lint from his sleeve before sliding one elegant hand into the pocket of his bespoke suit. "Won't you at least consider? Perhaps you should like a mate, after all."

"I should like to be left the hell alone," Anwar growled. There was nothing worse than being told what to do. He had been able to skirt the Order of Immortals for years, along with their meddlesome ways. Anwar was nothing more than a victim of Constantine's folly. He could curse him if he hadn't been tucked in tight to his hundred years' sleep. "There are a million things I'd rather be doing than getting tied down to some dunder-headed female for the sake of appearances. It's as if the Order believes it is still relevant, but its methods and ways are obsolete. Most of the cultures don't seek its gover-nance. Instead of steeping in old accords, it should be forging new relevance in a society that sees its council members as no more than figureheads."

Seated at his father's desk, Anwar felt the exact same as the day his entire race, a lot of fifteen who remained, had accepted they could never return to their homeland due to the witch's curse. For two centuries, they'd walked alone, stripped of their riches and wealth. They could not repopulate their race, and anytime they tried, their chosen mates suffered fates worse than death—to never see the sun again and to be forced to live on the blood of others. To prevent them from ever ascending to the seat of power once enjoyed by Atlanteans, and as punishment for their selfish ways, any who blood-mated would have their strength divided—split between the two. In order for them to survive, joining the Order had been necessary. In fact, the Atlanteans had been present to help draft the accords.

And so, his life as Anwar Tsedek, Atlantean prince, earth dweller, began. His life had been glamorous, albeit cautiously lived so as not to alert the humans. As biological parents of the vampires, Atlanteans had all the same skills but could walk in daylight. The rules of the accord allowed the remaining Atlanteans to have mates from other races, given their dwindling numbers. Most of the supernatural races knew nothing of the Atlanteans' ancestry, nor the deadly secrets that could harm his kind. Of course, no one knew Atlanteans were the responsible parties behind vampire origins, either. Yet another secret kept by the Order.

"Well, at least they aren't forcing you to accept a mate. You can choose your own, you know. Eire is the easy choice, but I understand your rationale." Mael picked up the tablet from the table where he'd just been seated and brought it across to Anwar. The screen was paused on a video. When Anwar didn't accept what was proffered, he laid it gently on the desk. "Drink? I think it may tamp down some of your ire. For my sake." He turned away, heading to his favorite part of the décor—the wall-to-wall bar stocked so well, it looked like a liquor store.

Anwar simply waved his hand before allowing his eyes to lower to the screen in front of him. There was a pleasant enough female frozen in position with a large arrow right in the center of her face. Her eyes were almond-shaped and luminous, even in their natural color. When vampires were aroused or excited, the eye shade could change to virtually any color in the world, much the same as Atlanteans. For Anwar, his normal was a whiskey coloring, which transformed into a vibrant blue hue. Mael's were red—one would think it was a direct contradiction since he was a fallen angel, but then again, most had never seen him angry. In fact, Anwar thought himself the only one skilled enough to make him so. "Who is this?"

Mael glanced over his shoulder from his position at the bar, a smirk lifting the corner of his mouth. "That is Farrah Grant. She's one of the owners. They have an interesting mission statement. One I thought you'd take a liking to." He returned his attention to one of his concoctions. It was either an old-fashioned or a Manhattan. He'd taken a liking to whiskey and bourbon in the late 1820s and never quite gotten over it. Both drinks came out at the turn of the previous century... or perhaps even later—who could remember such things when you got to be their ages? "Hit play, Anwar. You can't just *will* on electronics."

Anwar didn't care whether his sigh was audible. Mael wasn't the constituency, therefore there was no need to put on airs. He was a friend and had been for years. "This is not an agreement to throw myself into the fire. I'm just curious. Don't get any ideas." He pressed the button, and the image onscreen became animated.

*"Hi. I'm Farrah Grant, owner of the Vampire Match-making Agency, and if you're here, you're probably interested in finding your forever mate..."* As if to reassure the viewer, a wide smile spread across her lips. Red lipstick accented her mahogany skin. An unreasonable urge to ruin every part of her with his seed stirred to life.

Anwar hit the screen, forcing this Farrah Grant to freeze in a rather awkward position—her full lips made the perfect O. Under normal circumstances, he would have chalked that up to the woman on the screen's victimization by technology. However, these were not normal circumstances since his *kensee* stirred straight to his cock. His *kensee*, known to awaken when a potential mate was present, was the first sign that he should not—no, would not—go down that path with the female.

Mating was overrated. The overwhelming need to protect your mate at all costs, the split of power, the blind allegiance to their mate's cause, all of it. If a bullet were shot at someone, Anwar would of course help in those circumstances, but mating could make you step *in front of* the bullet. Was he ready for that?

"Hell no." Long ago, he'd resolved that if he were to be forced to mate, it would not be with someone he felt anything for—love, lust, or hate. Generally, the females he met gravitated near the loathing axis. But this one... She made him *feel.* The mere notion scared him more than anything.

"Look, you haven't even given it a chance." Mael returned, placing the fragrant cocktail on the desk two inches in front of Anwar. Sugar cubes and cherries resolved the guesses on which drink he'd made. "It's either this or Eire, and I don't believe you would want that." With a shudder, he took his drink back to his previous seat and elegantly sank into the wing-backed softness.

"Honestly, which is worse? Playing this dating game or selecting Tarik's chaste daughter?"

"Come now, you know the answer to that. With VMA, you—"

"What is VMA?" Anwar knew but couldn't help being a dick about it.

"Vampire Matchmaking Agency. You just heard her say it." Mael shook his head. "As I was saying, they swear by their services. They've made hundreds of matches in the three years they've been in business. The method seems efficient, and most every single female among the species has signed up. It's like... what is it the humans say? Shooting into a barrel, or something like that." He took a deep drag of cocktail, then swirled the drink. The squared ice cube snapped apart in the glass as it melted.

Anwar rolled his eyes before returning his attention to this Farrah. She was pretty, though not his normal type. In fact, Anwar had never seen another female with more ordinary features that were quite so exciting. Dropping the iPad back on the desk, he grunted.

The fact that he wasn't ready to mate, even after the last available Atlantean had been snapped up, was telling. Either it was them, or... Maybe it was him? He hadn't so much as thought of bonding to any of the females he'd fucked in the past. Then there was Tarik's daughter, Eire. She was a faerie, and besides the terrifying rituals of her race, she was undoubtedly vapid.

A slew of women from his past, and none of them had been his *forever mate* as this Farrah person implied was out there, just waiting for him. But it could have been that he just didn't want to be with someone for the long haul. "Why would anyone want to shoot into a barrel?" he asked, taking a drink.

"In order to preserve Atlanteans, you must take a mate prior to the next grand assembly. Otherwise, your race will perish. This isn't news to you."

Anwar knew the reasons and the rules. His father had written most of them. And he knew very well why. Mating was essential for their race when so few of them existed. Any mate counted as representation. Sixteen was the magic number if a race wanted to maintain their seat in the Order. When Emile had lost his life last year as a result of a hunter attack, it left the Atlanteans vulnerable. Emile's blooded mate, Syriah, was in mourning, leaving her unavailable for five years. As the only unmated male, it fell to Anwar.

For the first time, he wished he were Mael. He was free to do as he wanted. There were no rules assigned to him. He'd truly hit the gene pool lottery. He was an angel, the only one who'd fallen in thousands of years, and therefore held no seat in the Order.

"This is bullshit." The one good thing about humans was their curse words.

"Be that as it may, we need to get you mated. Preferably quickly. Your entire lineage could be at risk."

As much as Anwar hated it, regardless of their abilities, Atlanteans would once again lose their homes and everything they had if they lost their position in the food chain. Only fifteen of them left since Emile had been murdered. Fortunately, the existence of hunters had diminished greatly in the last decade.

Sixteen were needed, however, and it was up to him.

Immortality was fine. Being servants to the other races, if he and his kind were lucky, was not something his father would appreciate. "Fine... fucking fine or whatever."

He stared down at the screen again, still puzzled by the innocence in those eyes. There was no way she was anything like the rest of the vampire females. While Anwar wondered why he would have even been concerned if she was, he hit the play button.

*Here at VMA, we use every aspect of your preferences to find your ideal mate. From blood-type selection to specific skills and abilities. Take a look at our sample profile...*

Her voice was soothing, as well. As he leaned back in his seat and listened to her melodic tone, one thing kept coming back to him, again and again.

*How the hell will I get out of this mess?*

CHAPTER THREE



The level of fear in the room made Mael's heightened senses flare. The strongest representatives from every race were present, save the Atlanteans, for obvious reasons. Whenever one entered the Order's conclave, the building itself served as a ring of protection from harm, and despite their agreements and forged alliances, no race trusted another.

To make matters worse, Mael was an angel. There were no wards or charms to save any of them from his gifts. Falling from Heaven didn't strip you of them, only kept you from reentering the proverbial pearly gates. Hence, Lucifer's reign in Hell.

Each member of the Order was very well versed in Mael's many skills and traits. What they feared was what they didn't know. For centuries, Mael got by on that. Until they'd threatened the one thing he had no control over.

"I trust you have convinced him?" Viktoria, a vampire and the illustrious leader of the Order, broke the tension first, because of course she would.

She was a two-thousand-year-old murderer. Unlike most counsels, which took to their seats during meetings, the members of the Order stood for the entirety of their gatherings. Mael could see every bend and curve of her body. Long, flowing blond hair spilled over her shoulders and down the front of her, curling on the ends around what the humans would consider a perfect set of breasts. Everything was on display in a long, black gown cut nearly to her navel. Olive-toned skin and a muscular physique made her desired by every male, and a few of the females, in the belly of their cave, while her acrid, depraved heart had made her their leader.

"As I promised, Anwar will consider meeting the girl."

"I didn't ask you to get him to consider. I told you to make him comply with our wishes." Her calm voice was tipped in glacier-hard ice.

"I can only reason with him. I've told him." Mael stepped forward into the glowing circle. The cave was filled with some of the earth's elements and a representative mineral that neutralized each race's powers. Silver for vampires, iron for shifters and lead—more specifically, a stake made of such—could pierce the heart of a fae and kill them. Then, there was steel for the orcs. Thankfully for each of them, there were no other fallen archangels, because nothing would stop them. Fallen angels were affected by iron to some degree.

And, surprisingly, very few had fallen since there were only a few rules they needed to follow. The first of them being, do not interfere with the lives of God's most precious beings—his humans.

Angels were the only creatures able to procreate, aside from the humans. And Mael's brother, Azazel the Archangel, had abused his privileges, then been held up as an example of what not to do. To create a Nephilim was a cardinal Enochian sin, and Azazel and his lover had been lain low for their sins. Mael had turned his back on his own love to watch over Azazel's child and had then lost the use of his wings for his loyalty to his brother cast out of Heaven. As a final blow, the feathers of Mael's wings had been tipped in iron to make flying difficult and to represent his mortal crimes. He'd never regretted his loyalty to Azazel, but his love... well, that was something he hoped to one day remedy.

As long as the angel Azazel's offspring never exhibited powers, the archangels would allow her to remain alive. She had exhibited powers, though, hadn't she? And Mael had gone to extraordinary lengths to hide Lelania's ability to manipulate time from the archangels, using his own light signature as a mask.

And now Viktoria knew what he'd done and was blackmailing him. As long as he did what Viktoria wanted, he wouldn't have to reckon with the additional consequences of his actions for a great while.

"Not good enough, Mael," Viktoria snapped. "We need a reason to cast Anwar and his father out of the Order. If that isn't simple enough for you to comprehend, let me make it easier. If you do not return here with results as we agreed, we will have no choice but to assume you cannot. He is to remain in the dark until we have proof that he's willfully broken the accords. The proof needs to be irrefutable so there is no mistaking it. I can't take power from the Atlanteans without it. And not that I need to remind you, but you do know the consequences of failure, do you not?"

Through clenched teeth, Mael released a low, growling hiss. "I cannot simply possess him and do as you wish. There are limitations, even for me."

"You see"—Viktoria began a slow, deliberate pace to the center of the circle—"I don't really care about your limitations. There are tactics we can take to make this easier for you. Each of us has a specific set of sk—"

"Don't you dare quote that movie, Viktoria." Mael hated her proclivity of stealing references from pop culture. For someone who claimed they hated humans as much as she did, she certainly appropriated the fuck out of their culture.

She stopped just inches before him. "Let's see... I hold all the cards and you *don't dare* me? I think you are confused on the balance of power, Mael."

"No, I am not confused. You are a bully. The remainder of the Order's members are your flunkies and too afraid of you to challenge you. One day, though, they'll find a weakness. Rest assured, they will exploit the fuck out of it when they do." Mael was barely holding on to his control. The only thing that barred him from tearing her limb from limb was her awareness of his interventions on behalf of his charge.

Protecting Lani had caused him to lose the love of his life, to lie to Constantine and Anwar when they'd given him some purpose in his endless life on earth, and to fall into bed with the likes of Viktoria. The archangels would never understand his rationale for doing any of those things, for their allegiances were never to one another. Were it not for Azazel saving Mael's life, Mael may not have been able to fathom his betrayal of their brethren. It was what made him and Azazel truly brothers—the fact that each of them would lay their lives down for the other. Azazel had saved Mael, taking a blade through his flank to protect him. While it was ages ago, when wars with demons were common and the stories of the Old Testament were born, Mael had kept his promise and watched over Azazel's most precious gift.

He stepped forward, fists clenched at his sides, and hanging on to the barest of constraint.

"Even if what you say is true, who, exactly, is going to check me on it? And remember, he's to be in the dark, so we can expel his kind once and for all." A menacing smile spread over Viktoria's extended, threatening fangs.

## CHAPTER FOUR

The rush of clientele had come almost too fast and hadn't stopped since the VMA had hung out its awning. Every unmated, horny creature in North America seemed to have heard about the dating service. No need to muck shit up with some fancy name. Vampire Matchmaking Agency *was* pretty much it.

Farrah could almost hear Leila's warnings on keeping things lowkey. She was small fries, though. There were so many other shady vampire practices going on, would they bother with her? Probably not. At least, she hoped not.

The guise of the furniture store explained the taxes she paid. They wouldn't want to ruin such an excellent cash cow. The Order's greed was essentially what saved VMA from being discovered. Farrah hoped she could keep it that way.

"Thank you for calling VMA, where your next bite could be forever. How can I help you?" The call came in on the designated cell phone for VMA, so there was no confusion on which business they were looking for. Referrals were through friends, and thanks to Ennis, her tech god, the VMA was in the darkest parts of the web.

Farrah waited for the caller to ask a bunch of questions about the app, the primary mode of use for clients. Even with this awareness, there was no motivation for her to learn how it all worked. All that could go to Ennis.

"Hello... um, I'm supposed to meet someone, and they haven't showed." The voice on the other end could have been any male client with a date that evening, but she had an idea even before she started the verification process. Placing the phone on the counter, she tapped the caller's number into the database's profile search engine. Within moments, a correlation was found in one of the profiles.

"Mr. Hammond?" The question was a moot point, but still...

"I don't know how you can tell it's me... No one else from Baton Rouge, yah?"

"No, it's the puppy. I can always hear her in the background." She laughed.

"Oh, I never go anywhere without my Bella," he said. "Isn't that right, you little sweetie pie?" To which the excitable shih tzu barked.

"I wouldn't, either. So, let's see what happened. If your date contacted us through the app to cancel, I can see it on my end." Anytime someone got a bit nervous over meeting a stranger or whatever the reason, Farrah knew. Most of the time, she didn't have to play investigative reporter, though, because each client received a cancellation notice. But, Mr. Levell Hammond, who had the image of Pixar's *Pets'* animated cast as his profile pic, refused to check his app. He preferred telephoning. She tapped at the keyboard, bringing up the event—code for date in her homegrown system—and found... nothing.

Not that Mr. Hammond hadn't been stood up before, but given the costs associated with VMA, standing someone up without notice moved the offender to the bottom of the list. "I don't know, Mr. Hammond. It doesn't look like Violet sent in a cancellation request. Did you two discuss the location?"

"Oh, we did. And she seemed enthused by the prospect. Maybe I should give her a nudge in the app? I mean, maybe she realized I'm just an old geezer and she changed her mind..."

"Well, I doubt that. You're a spry five hundred and eleven. We've matched people twice your age."

"Yes, but I was turned late in life. You all look, at the oldest, thirty. I was fifty-seven the day I transitioned."

"We pride ourselves in catering to the open-minded. And fifty-seven-year-old humans still have full, happy lives. It will be no different for you, Mr. Hammond. Now, I'll go and see if I can connect with Violet. And you reach out to her. It wouldn't be the first time wires have been crossed."

"All right. I'll message her as soon as I stop feeling sorry for myself."

"Indeed. No pity parties. I'll speak to you soon."

"Okay, bye now."

Farrah clicked the earpiece of her headset to end the call and immediately fired off a message to Violet. It didn't make sense. They were truly a perfect match. Besides that, it wasn't like Violet to miss anything. She was always early. It wasn't that Farrah knew everything about her, but she had known her long enough to identify something out of character.

Since it was mere hours before dawn, Farrah decided to begin the system reboot recommended by Ennis. The popularity of the agency had soared in the past year to a level she hadn't particularly expected. She had clients of nearly every race included in her database. As such, when she'd set up her app and website, she hadn't invested in enough server space for the current demand. It was a tax on the system. Fortunately, Ennis was an expert at development and infrastructure. His skills saved Farrah from having to do anything drastic, like wipe her clients' profiles.

The whirring of the metal shutters, serving as both security and safe harbor from the sun in the event Farrah needed to stay over-day, had already started when the entrance bell sounded. Farrah brought her head up from the dashboard and found new arrivals that surely had to be lost. Was the one on the left... Thor? Zeus?

Seriously, he looked like a god. One that smelled of freshly smoked tobacco and vampire. His deep brown skin kissed with golden undertones was the perfect base for a chiseled jawline and hazelnut eyes. No way he'd come in to be matched or mated. A guy like that was probably loaded up to his ears in premium female. But a girl could hope, right?

Beside him was some guy who was equally shameless in his hotness. She wasn't sure what the other guy was, but she glanced around to ensure she wasn't being punk'd. "Um, may I help you? You looking for some furniture?" Perhaps they were a gorgeous couple furnishing their dream home on the riverfront just a few miles down the road, or some other idyllic scenario.

"No," the one with alabaster skin and fiery blue eyes said. "My name is Maelstrom, and we are interested in finding a mate for him." He pointed to his friend who, based on the ask, probably wasn't his lover.

For a moment, she froze, unsure of what exactly to say. When they just stood there, staring at her ineptitude, she startled back to herself, bringing her focus online. "I'm Farrah. Welcome to VMA." She walked around the desk and over to them in what she hoped was a smooth, sexy gait. She knew she'd fucked that up from the wobble in her ankle. A quick recovery aided by an heirloom lamp saved her from busting her ass. "And you are?"

She plastered on a smile in an effort to distract from her awkwardness, knowing full well she'd need a flying circus behind her for any hope of that. *Christ, why couldn't she be Leila? Just for this moment right here...* She stared at the man who had yet to be introduced. Now that he was closer, she saw him in his full glory. Full lips, dimples, broad shoulders. He was like a... the only thing coming to mind was his sex-on-a-stick persona. And boy oh boy, did she want at that stick like a golden lab in a wide-open dog park.

Taking her hand after what seemed like an eternity, he drawled, "I'm Anwar." His accent was one she couldn't place. Or maybe it was just that she was lost in his eyes. Their hands clasped together for probably a second too long, and she prayed her palms weren't sweaty.

She let her eyes graze over him for another few seconds that dragged out like hours. He was clad in black. Everything about him was a feast to the senses. He was badass and knew it well. The long-sleeved shirt clung to his muscles, and despite him having let her hand go moments earlier, she was still holding it out as if frozen in place.

There was something lecherous in her thoughts of him. She brought her eyes up to his and stuck her stubborn hands into the pockets of her jeans. The safe place of his face was no cakewalk either, but at least it wasn't a one-way ticket to hornyville. "So, Anwar, how can I do you... help you?" *Fuuuucccckkk it all...* Clearly, she had been slightly brain-damaged at the sight of him. If she could have snatched those wayward words from the air, she would have.

"Your voice... it's unique. What's that accent I hear?" Dammit to hell. He smiled for a moment and damn near blinded her.

She searched his face for a hint at his game. Something that would tell her whether he was full of shit or genuine. She still didn't buy that he needed help finding a mate. Nor the other one, who had so far, fallen into the background and been silent save the hasty intro. In all her life, every hot male she'd met was usually anything but kind and genuine. "Georgia. The state, not the country." She stifled a laugh, then tried to cover the extra seconds she'd taken to answer. Instead, it came out half snort, half cough, one hundred percent geeky.

"That's it, Georgia in your formative years and later on in your life, northern. Presumably here." He turned back to his friend, who gave him a shake of his head. "Anyway, this place finds mates, correct? I need one. Preferably this week."

There it was, the jerk in hiding come out to play. "Okay... um," she said, quickly recovering from her infatuation. No matter how good-looking a male was, mates should not be treated as if ordering from fast food. "That's not actually how this works. First, you would—"

"I honestly don't have time for all that." His words were clipped, and though he was asking her for consideration, he seemed to be giving her a demand.

Now that got her hackles up. There was no way he would barge into her place and demand she just freaking give him a girl. She didn't care about the way his lush locs slipped over his shoulders and ended at his flawless pectorals. Everything about him seemed to invite her to touch and explore. If only to see if he was real. "This isn't a brothel. My clients come here because they are seeking a life mate. Not someone to bone for the night."

"That's what I meant," he said, some of his smile fading. "I'm looking for my forever mate. I just need to do it tonight."

"Uh-huh. Sure, you are. If you're truly interested, you may visit us online and enter the "special orders" section of the website. Enter the pass phrase *dungeons and dragons two fang*. No spaces, no caps, and the number two. Complete the questionnaire and then if you match up in our compatibility profile, I will contact you, and we'll go from there." Farrah extracted a card from her pocket and handed it to him.

He didn't take it. Only stared at it like it she'd sneezed on it. "Do you realize who I am? I am a prince, ordained by the heavens. Anyone in your paltry profiles would be lucky to have me. My lineage can be traced back to the original six."

Liar... he had to be. He should have just added *peasant* on the end. "Uh-huh, I get it. No, I didn't know that, but it's no surprise. I always figured my first encounter with a royal would come when he is trolling for a princess through a *paltry* dating app. Now, if you don't mind, we are closed. I need to lock up, if you're all set, Your Majesty." Farrah looked between the both of them and fluttered her fingers in a wave of her hand to get them moving.

Anwar turned to look back at his companion. "Well, this was your idea..."

With a sly smile, Mael winked at Farrah, almost as if he were happy with something she'd done. "Yes, I am aware. Miss, I will take you up on your offer." Finally, he dragged his eyes away from her and trained them on his friend. "Let's go. We'll arrange a meeting with... Farrah, is it?" He glanced to her and, when she nodded, he was back at his testy buddy. "We'll come back and see your mate matches. I rather like the sound of that." While Anwar was giving her a full view of his back, she could tell he was snarling at Mael, who seemed so very elegant and refined.

"Thank you and have a wonderful night." She returned to the counter and hit the button to retract the shutters.

"And to you, as well," Mael said. "Oh, and should we need to contact you, shall we utilize the number on the card?" Anwar brushed past him and bumped his shoulder before stalking to the closed door. He paced back and forth as the shutter rose, and once it was done, he hit the exit door so hard, it banged back against the building before slamming shut. Thankfully, it had been made with reinforced, shatter-resistant glass.

Farrah just shook her head and returned her attention to Mael, who was picking up the last brochure on the counter. Normally she kept them behind the desk, in the off chance a human walked in. "Yes. Once he completes his profile, that is."

"You know, he really is a prince."

The other guy seemed like he was just being arrogant, but this Mael... as he spoke, it was as if she was wrapped in a blanket of security—of truth, of light, of warmth. She stared at the asshole's back through slitted eyes before returning her attention to Mr. Fuzzy Feelings. Weren't they the odd couple? "All he has to do i—"

Holding up a mild hand, he stopped her. "I understand there are rules. And at times, my friend is a bit irreverent of procedures. It's a whole thing, but the point is, Ms. Grant, we do need your help. And as petulant as *his highness* is, he actually is out of choices. Trust me, we'll follow the rules. I bid you good night." With a bow, Mael turned and exited behind his grumpy, maladjusted friend.

They both exited, and Farrah couldn't do anything but watch them go. The tall one with the gorgeous hair, perfect teeth, and luxurious locs flowing over broad shoulders looked refined and all, but he was obviously a jerk. It was proof that wealth had no bearing on class. *Dick...* At least she'd stood her ground, though. As long as she could help it, she would forever protect the hearts of her clients. It was just unfortunate this one had been so hot. As usual, it had been just her luck.

She headed into the back to bring out more brochures. Despite the attempt to carry on as usual, her mind flipped back to the features of Mister Steal-Your-Panties. He was stunning to look at with a rich, baritone voice that awakened things deep inside her. Ugh. So went the story of her life. She was an alpha-hole magnet. Luckily for Farrah, so much info was on social media about guys like him, she knew exactly what she was dealing with. Hell, a girl could diagnose every megalomaniacal, selfish, creepy dickwad down to the socks they preferred to wear just from watching TikTok. He wasn't what she should want. It was the exact reason she pushed him from her mind with thoughts of chocolate cake. Indulging in her favorite confections was the thing she missed most about being human. Food was harder to digest now. But a chocolate martini would hit the spot.

Returning to the front of the store, she bent to tuck the VMA brochures into a dark and hidden slot beneath the counter. She would simply push his ass out of her mind and go on about her business. It was the best course of—

Farrah screamed as she stood back up and found someone there. Her knees buckled, and she grabbed the ancient cash register, hoisting it above her head.

"Wait, Farrah... it's me, Eire!" The loud shriek was the only thing that saved Eire.

At the last second, Farrah managed to reposition her aim and, instead, dropped the three-dozen-pound monstrosity onto the floor. It smashed to the ground, bells ringing, and the cash drawer unceremoniously sliding across the floor and into the foot of a century-old curio. "Girl, I could have messed you up. How'd you get in here?" Farrah knew she hadn't heard the bells chime from the door. She would have heard them even in the back, thanks to her vampire hearing.

"I'm fae. We don't need to use doors. I'm so sorry about your cash drawer." In one elegant swoop, Eire retrieved the register and its wayward drawer then placed them on the counter.

"It's okay. Just... maybe announce yourself next time." Farrah touched her twisted-out 'fro to ensure the curls hadn't straightened from fright, since it felt like every hair stood on end.

"I'll remember that. And again, I'm so sorry." An apologetic wince went over her cherubic face. Farrah still couldn't imagine how she could be that gorgeous and need Farrah's help.

"Hey, it's okay. You just startled me is all. This isn't exactly the best neighborhood," she said with a roll of her eyes. Then she thought about it. "But what was with the disappearing act yesterday?"

Eire held her head down, averting Farrah's eyes. "I honestly can't risk anyone knowing I'm here. This place is already against the rules, and I have to say, my father's reach is long. If one of the fae folk saw me, they wouldn't hesitate to turn me over to him. For that type of information, even though they would have to break the rules themselves, they would still have all kinds of wealth bestowed upon them. We fae are a tad bit materialistic."

While Farrah didn't know Eire's father personally, she certainly had heard enough about the ways of the fae to know the assessment most likely true. Coupled with the mystique of the fae, there was also the old wives' tale that the fae were unable to lie when asked a direct question. "I understand. We can meet somewhere else if you like, or do it all by phone? Whatever makes you most comfortable..." As soon as she'd said it, Farrah heard all kinds of Leila-implanted warnings in the back of her mind.

"Oh, I guess I haven't... I guess I didn't think about it that far. I've only ever been able to rely on myself, you know?"

That part was foreign to Farrah. While being a vampire could be lonely, she had always had Leila. And before her death to the human world, she had had family she could depend on back in Georgia. Despite all that, she nodded in agreement. Empathy was something no one really needed personal experience to have. "I can lock the door if you like... we could dim the lights. I don't have other appointments tonight, so—"

"You would do that for me?" Eire looked up then, her eyes expectant and a bit wet with unshed tears.

"Of course. You're right. If your father is that high up in the Order, we should keep this on the down-low." Turning around, she pointed to a couch in the back of the store. "Go over there, and I'll just dim the lights and lock the door," Farrah said.

"Okay. And thank you so much... for your under-standing. Not many supernatural beings would care for my plight."

"No problem. Go on now," she said before mentally willing the lights down low and the lock on. Farrah and Leila had been careful not to use silver workings in any of the store's elements to ensure their skills could be used.

She grabbed her laptop and headed on back, but not before trying to tamp down the warning bells in her mind. While she was fully aware of the risks involved, she'd known going in that VMA was against the Order's accords. If all else failed, VMA was hardwired to self-destruct in the event of discovery. Farrah just hoped it wouldn't come to that. And who knows, since she'd never actually seen them punish anyone, maybe they'd changed their perspective?

nwar had been seething since he'd met that Farrah person in the flesh. How dare she be so callous and short with him. She'd been no bigger than a sprite. Of all the inconsiderate—

"Are you still lamenting, Anwar, or do you want to complete the profile?" Mael's intrusive voice cut into Anwar's thoughts.

"No. I would wish to be linked to that female's business no more than I would long to be drawn and quartered."

"To be fair," Mael said, stepping into Anwar's line of sight as he stared out over the pool and into the rising sun, "you did walk in and demand to be mated. What you viewed as disrespect were her standard business processes, and you showed little regard for the way she has her establishment set up."

"I did no such thing. I told her I needed a mate. I did not lie, nor did I speak to her in an offensive way. She is an infuriating little dictator." And so gorgeous, he'd dreamed about her for the last two nights. "Who says she would be able to find a mate for me, anyway? There wasn't a soul in the store. She was closing up at three a.m. like it was some sort of human bar." And her lips looked succulent. Anwar had visualized himself pulling her hair as he took her in every way she would allow him. His cock stirred as the images flickered to life in his mind.

"She is protecting her clients from harm. I would think you'd find it admirable. At least you know she had your best interests at heart." Mael exhaled a deep sigh and took the seat on the balcony next to Anwar. Leaning back, he kicked his heels up on the table in front of them and put both hands behind his head before staring off into the brilliance of the morning sky.

"I am in a hurry here." Pressing both palms into his eyes, he leaned his head back and ran a million different scenarios through his mind. The fate of his race depended on him stepping up and doing the right thing. Once he'd successfully pushed Farrah the Warden aside to get at the real issue.

"As much as I want to tell you this won't be a problem, I know Tarik. He won't be pleased. You'll be rejecting his daughter. It's simply not done. You need to have a good reason for doing so. Something like a blood-mate, maybe?"

"Listen, I've tried. I went to visit the nerdy librarian at her store, and she turned me away."

"Did you really, though? You seemed more bothered by her and the agency than anything."

"Don't be ridiculous. You saw me."

"All I know is that you asked for her help like you were ordering some popcorn at the movie theater."

Anwar snapped his head to the angel. Normally, they were in pretty fair sequence with one another. Obviously, that was not one of those times. "I was being straight-forward."

"Yup, if by straightforward, you mean being a flaccid dick, you've hit the bullseye." Grabbing the handle on the recliner, he lay back a bit farther in the chair and did not spare Anwar another glance.

"Fuck you, Mael. I've tried. I could call one of the Order members..." He thought about whether any of them would care about his plight, and the answer was a resounding no. "As much as I would hate it, I could call the bastards and accept the offer to mate Eire."

"After one shot, huh?"

"Farrah is not going to help. I can't see where I truly have a choice."

"I'm not sure how you so easily transferred from limp dick to pussy in so short a time. She did not say she wasn't going to help. She said there are procedures you must follow. Totally different things. If you pulled your head out of your ass for a second, you would understand what she was trying to tell you."

Anwar was set to curse Mael out, but nothing came out. He opened his mouth again, same intent. Still nothing. Turning away from him, he looked out over the sleepy morning streets of Detroit and watched as the humans began to make their way into jobs to start their monotonous days.

Mael was absolutely correct. Despite what Anwar chose to admit, his confrere had become someone he could rely on, indispensable to him. In this case, he would complete the goddamned survey. And then, the tiny sprite lady with her lovely dark hair, curves that should have come with a danger sign, and stunning smile would have to help him.

Despite this not being the plan, it would meet the ultimate goals of the Order. At least she wasn't one of the potential matches. There were a million females in the world. Someone like that could eventually have him wrapped up and whipped. That was the exact opposite of what he needed.

"Good rising. Thank you for calling the Vampire Matchmaking Agency, where tomorrow could be your forever."

Her jovial greeting made Anwar's lips quirk. It was as if she believed her own hype. Something told Anwar they did not share the same perspective on love and relationships. "Good evening. This is Anwar Tsedek. I should like to meet with you. I've completed your profile on the worldwide web and—"

The laughter coming from the other end stopped him short. "Oh, honey. There is no reason to be so formal. Sure, I can meet with you. When would you like to come in?"

"When are you free?" he said through clenched teeth. This Farrah vampire was beyond insufferable. Yet somehow, he could legitimately imagine sinking his cock so deep inside her it would touch her soul. How would she feel against his body? With a shake of his head, he tried to ward off the thoughts of her legs wrapped around his waist.

"Let's see. I have to get the liquor order tonight, covering for my maker. How about tomorrow?"

"How about I meet you at the liquor?"

"Pardon?"

Dammit, he wasn't making any sense. "You're getting

liquor somewhere. I can meet you there." He had no idea why this female refused to simply comply with his wishes. Matchmaking was supposed to be her job, but it seemed she wanted him to do the work. Maddening.

"Oh..." There was a long pause.

"Hello, are you there, Farrah Grant?" he barked into the receiver. The cell phone creaked under the pressure.

"Yeah, yeah. I'm here. I was just thinking about how this could work. All right. I'll be at Melody, it's in Harmony Park. I'll text you the address."

"My number is—"

"Yes, Anwar Tsedek. Your profile is in my database, and you just called me from your cell. I'll send over the address in a few. See you then."

Three tones sounded in his ear, and Anwar could have sworn she'd just... had she just hung up on him? Anwar held the phone out from his ear to see if it was true. Indeed, the call had ended. *Insufferable...*

"I've figured out why you're so flustered by this female, Anwar," Mael said.

Anwar had forgotten he was in the room. No doubt to make him go through with it. "I can't fathom why that wouldn't be obvious. She has been terse in her communi-cations with me each time I've spoken with her. Should not that be enough?" He placed the phone on his desk before he threw the damned thing.

"I don't think she's being terse. She's just relaxed, no doubt a newer vampire. I don't see that telltale tension in her eyes. But no, I disagree with you. It's that she doesn't fall all over you like every other female. Granted, perhaps that would be different if she knew you weren't actually a vampire, but somehow I doubt it." Mael swirled his ever-present old-fashioned in its cocktail glass.

"What? I hadn't noticed, nor have I been concerned with her attraction to me."

"Oh, now I know you're lying. If not, why are you standing there ruminating over your exchange?"

Anwar took an accounting of his current position. He was indeed standing, fists clenched, arms roped across his chest, jaw tense. But there was no way Mael was right. It was never his intention to be the all-powerful Anwar. He didn't expect females to lose their shit over him. Straightening and dropping open hands to his sides, he took a seat in his leather chair and scooted the seat closer to rest his hands on the table. He picked up the phone gently, so as not to look unhinged, and moved it to the side. "Don't be ridiculous."

"Yeah, you're right. This is all very normal. You always have to concentrate to keep from breaking your phone. At any rate, I'd like to tag along for this profile review. You know, see your matches. If for nothing more than shits and giggles." Mael snickered before taking a drag from his drink.

"Fine... the sooner we get this over with, the better. And don't look so fucking smug. You've been hanging around with humans too much. Angels are supposed to have humility."

"Who the hell told you that? We're the worst. At any rate, I'm off. See you tonight. Heading to soak up some more human culture." He set the drink on the table, straightened his pale blue suit lapels, and buttoned his jacket. "Despite the whole global-warming thing, they do have wonderful hobbies. Gonna get in a round of golf before your big dance. Wear something, I don't know... appealing. You apparently need all the help you can get." With a laugh, he faded into ether.

Anwar ran a hand through his locs, happy that Mael left because he could have committed an assault against the male. Fuck Maelstrom with his tattered wings. He was way off base. Standing, he moved across the room to stare out over the city as the sun set. As the bright orange ball kissed the horizon, he wondered what, exactly, he should wear.

## CHAPTER SIX

"Good rising, Leila."

"Farrah, you are by far the cheeriest vampire before feeding I've ever met."

"Well, that's not my fault. It's in my DNA. Besides, I've visited the feeders. It helps that I'm covering the bar today." *The feeders* were the scores of humans who were compelled to forget their donations. There was a rotation of them. It protected the identity of the vamps who enjoyed blood from the vein as opposed to the blood bags from the bank the Order owned. No one liked for *the man* to know where they were.

"Well, good for you. I prefer my beauty rest. Not that I got any today. I'm going to check on Isabella. No one has heard from her in weeks. She may be reclusive, but this is ridiculous."

"I remember, you'd mentioned. I'm all good here. That client I told you about? He's meeting me here. He's a stiff one. If he doesn't open his pompous mouth, though, he'll be an easy match. Looks like a cover model."

"Hmmm. You mean the typical vampire?"

Farrah glanced down at her iPad on the bar. It was open to his profile, and despite her having just uploaded it, there were twenty-seven likes on his page. "You'd think. He's atypical, though. Something about him. At any rate, he'll be here, and the sooner I can match him, the sooner I'll be done with his bougie ass."

"Well, no one ever told you jackasses didn't need love too. You'll win him over. I don't know a single vampire who doesn't like you."

"How about they don't even consider me? That's a whole lot different from liking someone."

"Oh honey, if they didn't like you, you would have known. They love being evil, so they wouldn't have missed a chance to flaunt their power and make your life miserable. It gets them off. Anyway, I'm heading out. I'll head there when I get a chance. Ciao for now."

"Bye, girl. And don't get into any trouble."

"You need to let your hair down a little, my friend."

"Umm hmm. See you soon." Farrah ended the call and returned her attention to Anwar's profile.

*Question 1: How do you like to spend your nights?*
*Answer: Alone and unbothered.*

Blllurrrgh. He was definitely going to be a hard sell. What if she just left his pic up on the site? But that wouldn't be fair to unsuspecting females or males looking for a match. Normally, she would add some anecdotal info to the caption based on the client's responses. No luck there. She'd reviewed his answers, and they were all leaning to the leave-me-the-fuck-alone side. Bless his heart.

A knock on the door brought her head up. She put the iPad down with one more look at the most gorgeous male in creation, possibly. Damn shame he was a dick.

The moment the door clicked into place after the delivery man, there was another knock. It was too early for the bartenders and staff to arrive since Melody didn't open until eight. Which meant only one thing.

"Coming." Farrah headed over to the door, smoothing down her sleek tresses along the way. She'd flat-ironed her hair and added a little red lip color. She didn't normally, unless she was going out, but the armor of looking fierce was needed to deal with Anwar. *Sure, Jan. That's why you wore the leather skirt and bustier too. You always change out of your sweats for males you hate.*

Holding open the door, she found Anwar looking just as good and surly as he had the first time they'd met. "My associate, Maelstrom, will be along shortly," he said. No hello, just something that almost sounded like a demand.

If he spoke like that in greeting, what did he do in bed? *None of your damned business, Ms.* "Sure, I'll leave the door unlocked for him." She stood there for a moment, right in his path waiting for his next words. What was with him, anyway?

"Um, may I enter?"

"You don't need permission to enter a vampire establishment, Anwar." She snorted. Sheesh. The reactions he provoked from her were getting a bit old.

"Perhaps not, but I would need you to move aside instead of mowing you down." His eyes narrowed to near slits as he surveyed her in a careful, measured manner. He was stooping to her. He had to be seven feet tall.

"Oh, yeah, right. Of course, I should. Please, won't you come in?" Just... She sighed and moved aside, then removed the locking mechanism on the door. When she turned around, her face hit full-on chest. "Ow." She jumped back too quickly and her back hit the door. "Damn," she said, rubbing her nose. Sweet Jesus, he smelled of pine and whiskey and reminded her of a tall, fine-ass camping trip. Oh hell. Muddled thoughts were the first sign. She needed to get him matched before she offered to mother his children, despite vampires not being able to procreate.

"Apologies. I did not mean to—well, stand so close to you." Pushing miles of woven locs back over his shoulder, he rubbed his neck then glanced around before returning his attention to her. "Where would you like me to sit?"

"Don't worry about it," she said, recovering, if only slightly. Stepping past him, she led the way to where she'd been working on some potential matches. "Follow me." First, she would need to get some better responses from him. Taking a seat, she patted the barstool next to her, then pulled her tablet over.

"Thank you," he said. When he sat, he almost didn't fit the barstool. She wasn't just thinking that because of her own small stature.

"You're welcome. So, I was looking at your profile, and boy howdy, do you need some warming up."

"I'm not cold," he replied, as dry as day-old pita bread.

"That's not... um..." Trying to hold in her laughter, she adjusted on the seat and scrolled to the answer portion of his profile. "You see here? The question was *What is your favorite position?*" She held the tablet over so he could see.

Anwar nodded, his face serious, brows knit. "Yes. My favorite position is *offense*." Pointing an elegant finger to the answer space, he ran it under the typed word. "It took a while for me to get the hang of American football, but now, I'm really into it."

"Yes, but, honey..." She flipped her eyes up to meet his. His furrowed brows and pressed thin lips showed genuine confusion. "You know this is sexual... the question is about sex." She poked her tongue into her cheek, which was supposed to resemble fellatio, even though it didn't, actually.

"Of course, it was a joke." Anwar sat straighter on his stool, somehow managing to look even more uncomfortable.

"Um, how old are you, if you don't mind me asking?"

"I'm..." He paused for a moment, almost as if he... he didn't know? "What possible difference could that make?"

"Well, I find that people from the same era enjoy meeting and connecting. It makes the match more pleasant. And I saw"—she scrolled up to the age section and held it over to him—"you'd left this blank."

"Yes, well... you may enter nineteenth century." Anwar pushed it back in her direction with an open hand.

"Somehow I doubt that... I thought females were the ones sensitive about our ages."

"My, how very sexist of you."

"Well, I was turned in the eighties, so sue me. Let's move on. What's your favorite hobby? It was another blank question."

"Well, I can do this one thing. Would you like me to demonstrate?"

Farrah returned her attention to him once again. He had a way of not only staring at her but seeing inside her soul. It was a look that left her feeling ravaged by him.

"Yup. Let's see what you've got." He didn't seem to notice her very Freudian slip, and she hoped it stayed that way.

After unfolding his long body from the stool, he stepped around the bar and began gathering ingredients. "Once, a very long time ago, I enjoyed entertaining. This meant I was prone to need cocktails. I learned to make a very good old-fashioned. I should ask. Do you drink?"

"I do," she said, putting the tablet down and watching as he moved around as if he were the king of the castle, sliding over jars, taking bitters down, pulling highballs from their designated area. Shit, Farrah had been in that bar a million times and didn't know where most of the supplies were.

When he was done collecting items, he slid a highball in front of her. "Allow me to fill your vessel."

Yup, she was being fucked. Only between her ears. Everything in and around her core pulsed. Crossing her legs to keep her lady parts in check, she leaned forward, careful to cover her tightened nipples. "Okay, bud."

Who the hell responded like that? She did, apparently, when a male pushed her buttons.

"Right. So, the first thing is muddled cherries." Anwar opened the jar and extracted one with his bare fingers and held it up. "I prefer the expensive kind, such as these. Instead of being weighed down by preservatives, these are plump... firm. They don't dissolve and muddy the flavor until the right moment." He held the dripping fruit to his lips and ran the flesh over his extended tongue. "Then, when you're done with the cocktail, the fruit will have been infused with alcohol and you pop it into your mouth for an explosion of its sweetness." Anwar took the deep red orb into his mouth and chewed.

Farrah's fangs practically ejected just as every part of

her tensed. "Oh dear God," she said, covering her mouth with her hand.

Dangerously sexy eyes met her own, and she sat there, still and waiting for him to release her from his alluring web.

"Then, you go on to ice. I prefer one large—"

"Hello, kids. How are we doing?"

Farrah had never been so happy to be interrupted. With some effort, she coaxed her fangs back in, ignoring the urge to take a bite out of Anwar. "Hi," she said, swiveling on her stool, despite not knowing even remotely who it was that had just saved her from stripping off all her clothes and throwing her naked body onto the bar.

"Hello there. From your tone, I trust all is well." It was Anwar's friend, Malice? Malone? Farrah couldn't recall his name, nor anything else at the moment.

"Mael, perfect timing. I was just making Farrah and myself a drink. She wanted to know what I did," Anwar said.

She still hadn't worked up the nerve to turn back around and face him.

That's right, his name was Maelstrom. "How are you today?" she asked, stalling like the coward she was. If only for another minute or two.

Mael stopped in his tracks. He looked to her with a tilted head, then just past her to the bar. A look of realization dawned on his face, the slightly parted lips transitioning into a smile. "I see. Sweetheart, did he do the cherry thing on you?"

"Huh?" It was really all she could muster.

"Yes, well, I taught him that. Trust me, he learned all his moves from me." Mael started toward them once again. When he got there, he hopped onto the stool previously occupied by Anwar. "Make me one too, would you? And I like mine more bitter than sweet." He shifted in her direction. "So, how far have we gotten? I should tell you, the only way he keeps me around is a stocked bar and his inability to resist banter."

Farrah snickered, finally able to face Anwar again. "We got to his responses on the profile. I'm struggling to find suitable mates for him because he... Well, he... Why don't you take a look?" She held the tablet out to Mael, fingers quickly scrolling through the form, then shifted slightly to see if Anwar would object.

His shoulders lifted slightly, then fell, which she took to mean he didn't mind. Then he kept right on making those drinks. Fine by Farrah, since she really needed one.

Mael, having taken the tablet and begun scrolling, started making groans and guffaws. "Oh, my word. This is worse than I thought. Do me a favor, Little Bit, if I may call you that?"

"Um, no," Farrah said, fully over short jokes after hearing them her whole life.

"Suit yourself. Could you take me to a fresh profile? I know everything about the guy. I'll complete it. You can run it through your thingymabob, and bingo, we'll get him hooked up. Although, if I were him, I would have taken one look at you and wouldn't have needed a profile."

"Your drink." Anwar slammed the cocktail down and pushed it toward him so hard the liquid sloshed and spilled as it hit Mael's hand.

"Testy, huh?" Mael rolled his eyes back toward Farrah and leaned over. "He gets a bit cranky when someone tries to play in his sandbox."

Before Farrah could respond, Anwar cut in. "I do not

have a sandbox here, but if I did, those raggedy-ass wings would be in shreds."

An angel. Farrah had known Mael wasn't a vampire. But she hadn't ever encountered a being quite like him. Now, she knew. She would have never guessed they'd be so sarcastic. "So, now that all the testosterone is on display, can we get back to the reason we're here? Anwar, I should add 'libation slinger' to your profile."

Anwar brought his eyes back to hers. The malice drained from them, they were back to a gentle, molten brown. "How about gourmet libation slinger? You should taste it first, though. May I fill your vessel?" he asked, sending a shiver through Farrah. He had quite a way with words. After her barely managed nod, he poured the mix into another highball glass and placed it before her. "Wouldn't want to make you into a liar."

She picked up the glass and swirled it lightly, allowing the whiskey and faint cherry scent to linger in her nose before taking a sip. "Jeez," she said, wiping a bit of liquor from her mouth, "this is fantastic. Yes. I'll add it. What female doesn't want someone who will ply them with alcohol?"

"As charming as all that is, why don't you add he enjoys traveling and spending lazy afternoons in bed?" Mael added.

She moaned as the mixture hit her palate. Damn, he was good at it, after all. Reluctantly, Farrah lowered her glass. "Yeah, okay. That does sound better."

"Um-hmm. Thought it might," Mael added with a laugh.

Without warning, something streaked by the three of them. In a double-take, Farrah looked around to find what had created the breeze. It was Leila, surprisingly, since she never used her vampire speed. One second she wasn't there, and the next, she was at the front of the bar, standing beside Anwar and glaring rather maliciously at Mael. *Okay...*

"Just what the fuck are you doing in my bar?"

Farrah cleared her throat, hoping to crack some of the ice formed between the four of them. "Um... we were just doing my client's profile. Remember? I told you we would be here to—"

"Not you two. Him." She jabbed a stop-sign-red painted fingernail at Mael's chest, only stopping due to the obstruction of the bar. Farrah didn't want to think of what would have happened had it not been keeping them apart. She probably would have stabbed him in the chest.

"Leila," Mael gasped. It was the only time he'd ever seemed at a loss for words.

It was also the first time she'd ever seen Leila in a full-fanged murder look when she wasn't being threatened. Inches from Mael's face, she snarled, revealing dagger-sharp fangs. Whatever was happening between those two, Farrah wished she wasn't there to see it.

CHAPTER SEVEN

*T*he larger man's strong, corded arm went around her waist, lucky for that fucking angel, because she would have been on his ass like a bad suit. "I want you the hell out of here," she demanded. After a century, to callously sit in her place of business drinking her liquor?

Mael held both hands up and leaned back just beyond her reach. "Leila, I would have—"

"Yeah, whatever you would have. You know now, so I want you to pack your shit up and leave in the next five seconds, or nothing will keep me from tearing you limb from limb." She meant it too—despite the rush coursing through her, the scent of his woodsy cologne combined with literal heaven, and the fact that he was somehow even more devastating than the last time she'd seen him. He had been everything she'd thought she wanted. He was someone who hurt her so badly, she hadn't even mentioned him to Farrah. In all those years, she had buried the memory of him in a tinderbox beneath her soul. Because fuck the muthafucker.

"The last thing I want to do is cause you pain." He hadn't moved yet. His gray eyes were paler than she remembered, etched in agony. There was something deeper in them than she recalled.

Perhaps it was all the years, but she wasn't as angry as she once was. Now, she only wanted to kill him. Before, she'd had a million torture ideas, creatively crafted to cause eons of pain before a slow, agonizing death. "Hmph. That's a new one. I've got news for you. I don't care about the first, the second, nor the last of your things. I want you out of my sight and out of my goddamn bar."

"All right," he said, unfolding to his full six-feet-six-inch height. He was a masterpiece of masculinity. Too bad he was a shitty male. The stoic look was almost out of place, and so very different than the normal smirk he wore. "I would like to tell you before I go that I'm sorry. I was a different male then. One who had my priorities all jacked up. If y—"

Unable to bear the hundred-year-late excuses, what-ever they may have been, she held up a hand to put a halt to his lame attempt. "Save it, bro. I'm not in the mood. Don't let the doorknob hit you in the ass on the way out."

His head dropped, and he slowly shook it side to side, as if he were the one being wronged. "Okay, I'm leaving. Hopefully one day we can talk through it so you finally get to hear my side of things."

On a surge of adrenaline, frustration, and a freshly ripped hole in her heart, she lunged forward before the big jackass who had been holding her back could catch her. Picking up the half-filled cocktail glass, she flung it at

Mael as hard as she could. The liquid spilled as it sailed dangerously close to his cranium. With Mael's elegant and infuriating sidestep, it just missed him, continued, and smashed against the far wall. Mael turned slightly, glancing at the shattered glass before returning his attention to her. "You still have great aim. Take care, and Anwar..." He broke eye contact with Leila to look at the absolute giant to her left and nodded. "I'll catch you back at the penthouse, yeah?" Instead of waiting for a response, he turned and headed out of the bar. Despite her attempted assault, the damned angel didn't seem bothered in the least. He strolled out, elegant in a tailored suit that seemed cut for his body and his alone.

For a moment, Leila forgot about the two souls beside her, who looked beyond bewildered, and was lost in the part of herself that she'd put behind her. The two of them had been perfect. They'd made love on beaches all over the world, and he'd whisked her away, opening her eyes to things she'd never seen. But when his boss had come calling, he'd left her high and dry. Maybe it was stupid to think he could turn his back on Heaven for her.

A tear dropped on her hand when she hadn't even known she'd been crying. Oh, that would never do. "If you two will excuse me, I need to get ready to open."

"Leila," Farrah said, leaning forward and resting a hand atop Leila's, "if you need me to handle things here tonight, I will."

"No, don't be silly. Every now and again, the past comes back to nip at your heels. He's not the first lover I've accosted on sight. Won't be the last. No, you and Mister..." She turned to find Mael's friend and wondered for a moment if he was as big an asshole as Mael.

"I'm Anwar. I'm a client of VMA." He gave her a

slight bow, a mischievous glint in his eye. "And if I may say so, that is the first time I've seen Mael so humbled. If it's any consolation at all, I'd say you won that round."

Leila let a light chuckle escape. "Oh, honey. That wasn't even my best work. Now, if you two will excuse me —" With a nod to both of them, she skirted Anwar and headed for the back to pull herself together. Her Regency upbringing would not allow her to fall to pieces in public, no matter how long ago.

There was silence behind her as she walked away. She knew she would have to explain the whole ugly story to Farrah one day. Just not today, if she could help it.

Eire was right on time with her call. Once Farrah had shared how discreet the agency was, Eire had been willing to break her rule of only meeting in person. It truly was the best alternative for her. Farrah answered the VMA line by the second ring, even though she had to dash from the door. She hadn't told Leila about working with an Order member's daughter. It was the last thing Leila needed to deal with after her blowup with Mael.

"Hi there, Eire," she said.

"Um, hi. Is this... still a good time?"

"Of course. I trust you found the profiles I sent over to your liking?"

"I did. They were all so..." She paused for another moment. Eire was a badass fae princess, but for some reason, she was so unsure of herself. "Well, to be honest, they were very handsome. I didn't know what to expect."

"I'm glad to hear that. Were you able to set up a chat for any males you were interested in, or do you need help narrowing down?" Farrah took a seat behind the counter. She hadn't turned on any lights in the event Leila happened by on her way home from the bar.

"I was able to and chose a couple to get started. There's one who I discussed meeting up with this weekend. He's a shifter. I think he might be an appropriate mate."

"Well, let's take this one step at a time. First dating, then mating. You know? You'll want to treat this like an interview at first. While our algorithm does a great job with matches, nothing beats good old-fashioned face time."

"Yes, I agree." For the first time, Eire seemed to relax, letting out a breath as she said the words. "I will call you once we meet. He is taking me to a club in the city."

Farrah winced. Somehow, she couldn't see the elegant Eire in some club. "Have you ever been to a club, Eire?"

"Well, actually um... no. I'm open to exploring new things, however. I think I should have a great time."

Farrah couldn't help but smile at Eire's innocence. She hadn't been so optimistic in her own dating life. The algorithm seemed to work for everyone but herself. "That is wonderful. So, remember, if you need me, I'm just a call away."

"Yes, will do. I added my bank information into the account. It's under Mary Beth Streger."

Most of the supernatural community used human aliases. It was safer. Staying off the radar kept both humans and the Order out of your business. "Perfect. I hope you have the best time. Talk soon. Night to you. Oh, and please, check in on the app when you've arrived. It's just an added security feature."

"I will do that. And thank you, Farrah. For everything," Eire said. It was as if her smile could be heard over the phone.

As Farrah hung up, she got the familiar rush of endorphins from helping others find and hopefully keep love.

One day, maybe she would have her own. A part of her wanted to run a match between her and Anwar... but she'd decided against forcing through the comparison. It wasn't right for her to purposefully modify what was supposed to be an impartial process. Sure, she was in the database, but to interfere with the programming to specifically run her against his character traits was something she prohibited in the contract her clients signed.

Though her curiosity was piqued, her ethical side won out. If they were to match, it would be all coincidental, not something she forced. Farrah closed the laptop and tried her best to stave off the heart eyes she was about to sport.

CHAPTER EIGHT

The evening air was cool, a sharp chill rolling off the Detroit River despite it being a midsummer night. Five yachts, eight speedboats, and two cargo ships had passed by since he'd been sitting there. Three calls and four profile updates later, it was time for Anwar's date. Then it was past time. He'd waited at the River Walk until nearly midnight when the date had been scheduled for ten. Being stood up was something new for him.

He paced over to the railing. As the night dragged on, the wind had risen, and the sound of rolling waves crashing against the rocky shore grew more and more consistent. As much as he hadn't wanted to admit it, he was indeed on the receiving end of being ghosted. Instead of standing around with his vulnerability on display, he decided to go to the VMA. After all, it was her set-up, and if whoever this Lauren was couldn't live up to her end of the bargain after all his trouble, Farrah was going to hear about it.

She'd been unrelenting over the profile and the incessant need to fix him up. He was beginning to feel like *she* was his mate. Only without the fresh bloom of love. It was more like the later years when most of the petals had dried up and fallen to the earth. Given how she riled him so, he couldn't put his finger on the reason he wanted to ruin her romantic disillusionment in person. She was one who believed everyone should have some kind of fairy tale union. Anwar was just... well, he was a realist. Forever was a long time for immortals.

A quick sprint to the parking garage for his Porsche Cayenne, and he was at the VMA in practically no time. A light drizzle had started, so it was just as well he wasn't on his date since they had planned to walk around getting to know one another. Maybe grab some ice cream, which Anwar loathed, but Mael had insisted he try being amenable.

The furniture store-slash-dating agency was empty when he arrived, save an elderly vampire who was soaking up all of Farrah's attention. She had that laptop thing out and her hair was in a messy bun with a pencil stuck through the middle. Anwar let out a sigh. Only Farrah would use something that could technically kill vampires and spike it in her chignon.

He waited for a moment, glancing around at the various antique set-ups. Some of them reminded him of styles he'd seen throughout his lifetime. Furniture changed slower than clothing, so it was easy to mentally place the settees, paintings, and formal dining tables in order of era.

After a few seconds, he turned back to see if she was done with the octogenarian ten times over. Technically, so was Anwar. Perhaps it wasn't that the geezer was even talking to her. It was his demeanor. One thing Anwar knew about well was the ill intentions of males.

The easy candor between the two was enough to make him want to scream. All the giggling and laughing, the old male touching her and her not throttling the bastard raked against his skin.

He cleared his throat, making sure she heard him since he was standing closer than was proper when private discussions were occurring.

Farrah turned to face him, her wide smile never leaving as she nodded to him. Since she'd never smiled like that for him, he grew even more annoyed.

As if he knew Anwar was watching, the geezer rested his hand over Farrah's, technically her wrist, to draw her attention back to him. Maybe she was in a relationship... with that male? As far as Anwar could tell, she didn't mind that he was touching her. Why didn't she care that the old bastard's liver-spotted hands were on her flesh? Okay, maybe not liver spots, he thought. But for sure they were fucking old. Even worse, why did Anwar care if he had his hands on her? The liver spots that may or may not have been there were beside the point.

He had half a mind to storm out of the place, tell Maelstrom and the Order to shove it up their collective asses, and move on with his uncluttered, unbothered existence. Taking a seat instead of hovering over her, he made sure not to stare in their direction. Every neuron in his being was firing danger signals, blatantly advising him to get away from the female. She was a threat to his numbed-out existence. Anwar was beginning to feel. And not just normal feelings. Simultaneously, the tightening and ache of his sex made him aware of her every movement. Then there were her fangs... There was only one reason for them if one wasn't in battle. It was to eat. Whether it was dining during sex or not depended on the situation. Her fangs, his neck, her wet-looking mouth... it all added up. Since he wasn't there in pursuit of pleasure, the thoughts of her, and her sweet mouth, were just wrong.

The other female, her maker, walked over to her, wary eyes on Anwar. He hadn't even noticed she was there. Normally, he paid attention to everything, so to overlook someone else in the same building was different. Damn near strange. Heightened senses, including his sensitive hearing, should have prevented anyone from sneaking up on him. The fact that she had didn't escape his attention.

With a cocked brow announcing her suspicion, she leaned over to Farrah. "Why don't you let me take care of Mr. Batchelor's profile? I believe our other guest needs assistance so that he may get on his way... as soon as possible." Her syllables were drawn out, most likely with the express intent to shoot him a hint in the right direction. That direction being the street.

Anwar scented her distrust. It was thick in the air, like dark spices perfuming the atmosphere. He was used to people not trusting him. Someone had told him he had *dead* eyes. No light showed in them. If that was the case, his outside matched his inside.

Farrah looked at her, then in Anwar's direction with another nod. When she did, he felt he had no choice but to take his leave. No sense in making anyone uncomfortable. Not when he had so much he still needed to know.

His stiff member would have caused a problem, thus the only thing preventing the impending escape. So there he stayed. And goddamn if he didn't halfway enjoy it. Scared the shit out of him. He'd had sex about a dozen times in the last century. Hell, that was progress since he hadn't thought his cock would ever work again. He'd almost liked it the last time, even if he was still partially flaccid. Legit.

"Certainly. Go on, dear," the old vamp said through slightly extended fangs. He'd gotten a look at Leila and seemed happy to let her take over. She was just what most vampires liked. Which made Anwar even more of an outsider.

Leila and Farrah were an odd coupling for maker and progeny. For one, they were nothing alike. Most vampires didn't attempt to break the mold. It wasn't uncommon to see damn near doppelgängers in cases such as theirs. The similarities between Farrah and Leila seemed to stop at them both being females. Farrah had piles of hair that looked as if it would go on for miles when straightened and practically begged him to run his fingers through. The curls were drastic and voluminous. Anwar imagined pulling at it with both hands while taking her. He wiped away the cool beads of sweat that broke out over his forehead.

Leila was taller, skinnier, and had short, poker-straight hair. Her eyes were a liquid blue, nearly silver, void of almost all color until you got near the center of the iris. Farrah was curvy, her rounded physique one that would undoubtedly offer limitless pleasure. Farrah's eyes were beautiful, honey-brown orbs that made him wonder if they held the secrets of the world. Her maker... well, she was more angular. Nothing wrong with either of them, but while Leila was like most vampires, Farrah was like no other. Not human. Not angel. Not any other creature in the world.

"You're leaving, Mr. Tsedek?" The question Farrah asked was playful, especially near the end. She pulled the pencil out of her hair, and it fell over her bronze-kissed skin in waves. It was almost as if she wanted him to bed her, right there, in the middle of everything.

"You know, I didn't have an appointment." Anwar snapped his fingers as if it were merely an oversight, his charade blatantly obvious in his mind. He cursed his lack of professionalism but persisted, nonetheless. "It was not right of me to come in here without announcing myself first. Apologies." The words nearly choked him. He hadn't apologized in at least a century. And even then, under duress. As she drew ever closer, he struggled to hold her gaze and not look down at the breasts straining against the fabric of her T-shirt with the weird human saying *Better To Arrive Late Than Ugly*... Provocative, red-colored lips were beneath the words. They reminded him of Farrah's. Her thighs were the perfect shape to fit around his waist as he drove into her. Fuck. He needed to focus. It was exactly that type of bullshit that ended up becoming a distraction.

"No, it's no bother at all," she said. Anwar wanted to just turn and walk away. That was the reason he was standing and halfway across the spacious room. Because he was walking away. Right.

Beneath his skin, the prickling sensations grew more intense the closer she drew to him. With a deep breath, he struggled to compose himself. "It's just that... your client, I was supposed to meet? She didn't show tonight." Yeah, for his own good, he needed to get away.

Her movement was nearly undetectable with her fluid, lithe body. With a rush, she closed the distance between them, concern furrowing her brows. "What do you mean?"

The two most important parts of a male—his heart

and his cock—stirred as he watched her. He felt the burning, the igniting of a flame that would take more than a cold shower to extinguish. He should have been paying attention to what she was saying. "I was there, at the River Walk. We were to meet, then go to some ice cream place she knew about. And, well, she never showed. So I'm here to tell you maybe your algorithms are mixed up. Surely she's not looking for a mate if she stood me up." He smirked, waiting for her quip or saucy reply, which he'd come to enjoy during the time they'd spent together. Instead, the corners of her mouth tilted down and she darted around him.

Anwar turned to watch her. He hated seeing her upset. Sure, it was her responsibility to deal with the things keeping her clients from realizing their romantic aspirations, but she truly believed in her goals. He could see it in her furrowed brow, the look of concern creeping into her expression.

Once she made her way behind the counter, she picked up a smallish, dark gray card, pulled out her cell, and dialed. Before losing himself, he glanced around at Leila. She wasn't one to turn his back on. But he found her still diligently working with the old vamp. She was showing him some videos of females who were frankly out of his league. Well, there was no accounting for taste, and dude clearly had some bank. It was just the thing for a status-climbing newborn. They may even get off on centuries-old things. Like antiques. In his heart, Anwar knew he was being unfair. What he didn't understand was the sudden interest in a female to the point where he would mentally lambaste a male for simply touching her?

Farrah took the phone from her ear and replaced it in her pocket. "Lauren isn't answering."

"Well, maybe she had other plans. Honestly, it's not that serious. I was just coming by to mess with you before I headed home." Pressing her buttons was one thing, but he didn't want her to be overly concerned over a date he didn't give a damn about.

She placed the phone on the counter and stared at it for a minute as if she were waiting for a call. She looked so disturbed, he wanted to slip into her mind to see what she was thinking. That would be a violation, though, and he found he didn't want to do that to her, either.

"No, something's not right. Lauren has become a friend, and she was excited. Even after I warned her about your"—she waved her hand while searching for the word, still not looking at him—"dry sense of humor. She bought a new outfit for tonight." She walked around the counter and skirted him as she went along.

Before he could stop himself, he reached for her. The short sleeves of her shirt allowed him to feel that silky skin beneath his fingertips. He slid his hand down her forearm, then pulled her back to him. She turned to face him, her eyes wider, probably startled from his grabbing her. With one smooth motion, he pulled her hand to his lips and watched as a flicker came to life in her eyes. "It's all right. Maybe a better prospect came along? Don't worry. You know, vampires aren't exactly defenseless out there."

She cleared her throat and blinked several times. "You aren't the first person to be stood up in recent days. You don't have to wait here, though. I'll figure out what's going on and give you a call with another date or..." She hastily pulled her hand away from him... which annoyed the shit out of him. *Annoyed* probably was too light a word, but it was all he would let himself acknowledge. Everything was too goddamned real around Farrah. It was nothing he welcomed, nor needed.

"I see. I mean, I guess you're right. I'm here for a date, after all," he said.

"Right. So, we'll chat tomorrow, once I figure out what's happening."

He nodded, reluctantly. "Until tomorrow." Grabbing her hand, he lightly grazed it with his lips. He couldn't very well leave without kissing at least one part of her body. While she was distracted that evening, there would be another time when he could let her know that maybe his being stood up wasn't such a bad thing.

CHAPTER NINE

"Where'd the asshole come from?" Leila asked after both Anwar and Mr. Batchelor were gone, along with a couple of other newly interested clients who had gotten in before she could shut down. She'd even waited until they were locking the door at three a.m. to get to the club and hunt. That meant it was really weighing on her.

Farrah hadn't even mentioned the two additional clients who'd missed their dates. At the time, it seemed like an odd coincidence. Now, she wasn't so sure. "Who?" She twisted the deadbolt into place and waited on the street side to hear the beep of the alarm system arming. She turned, then winked and smiled at Leila before pushing past her.

"You know who," Leila said.

Continuing on her trek to lock down the shop, she focused on not placing too much emphasis on responses or reactions. She liked that dude but had sensed Leila's apprehension since running into Mael. She was always such a good judge of character, but sometimes, Farrah didn't want to do the right thing. She truly wanted to get Anwar mated, and after a few late-night calls, she was starting to want him mated to her. But the best interests of her clients had to take precedence over what she wanted for herself.

It felt good to lean into some pure animal attraction. She was damn near giddy inside from the simple touch. Hell, he hadn't even seemed interested until he pulled that handsy shit, and for all she knew, he could walk around kissing hands all the time. As gross as the possibility was, it could be true. Hard to reconcile being giddy over a kiss on the knuckles.

Tonight, she could have done without what she was about to say. Leila's nervousness had rolled off her in waves since seeing her old friend. And while she hadn't confessed what had gone down yet, her defenses were high, as evidenced by the impressive display of her fangs. *Stay away from suspicious characters like that.* Leila had a very real thing against males who wore their masculinity like armor. The alpha males, common in so many of the supernatural communities, were risky. Vampires hadn't survived as a species for thousands of years by being reckless—it was through calculation and cunning. Being bitterly ruthless was the order of the day. Couldn't be helped, but Leila's primary directive was to stay the hell away from that alpha shit.

After seeing her with Mael, Farrah had a little better understanding. Leila was very anti-mating. Her reaction to Mael made it clear that there was a lot of pain built up. Maybe one day, she would feel comfortable sharing.

"Forget about Anwar. I think we have a problem. Come look at this." Farrah headed over to the desktop and brought up files from the previous three weeks. "There have been"—she ran a finger over yellow spaces which were coded in the system to show a client's failure to make a scheduled date—"six missed dates in the past four weeks."

Leila walked around and looked at the computer. With a shrug, she pinned Farrah with a look of confusion. "Okay..."

"You know how many times that's happened in the past?" After Leila shook her head, Farrah continued, "Two. In the history of VMA, we've had two stand-ups. And both times, it was due to an untimely demise. And see here, those times there? That's how many times I sent automated calls to their phones asking them to call and reschedule. None of them have returned the calls. Something is happening."

Leila leaned in then. "Like... what do you think it could be?"

"I mean"—she sighed—"it could be nothing. Or maybe... they're being targeted? It's been females every time."

"That's a little—"

"Weird." Farrah grabbed the mouse and clicked on the hyperlinks to the individual profiles. She didn't know what she was looking for, but she knew something wasn't right. A sinking feeling hit her in the gut, and her mind tripped over a thousand different scenarios. "I mean, I guess I could see if there's some kind of software glitch? Maybe the females aren't receiving the messages from the app?"

"That could be. Why don't you give Ennis a call at rising tomorrow?"

"I think I will." She continued clicking through profiles, looking for something. Anything that would lead her to an answer, even if she didn't quite know the question.

"So, now can we talk about Anwar?"

"I kind of don't want to."

"Well, he keeps raggedy friends. And usually, birds of a feather fuck people over together."

"Since I'm setting him up with others, I don't know whether any of that is my concern."

"Well, just be wary of him. He is a whole lot of vampire to get over."

"I don't know what you could possibly mean by that," Farrah added, even if she knew perfectly well what Leila was implying. For a moment, she let her mind drift back to his fine physique and that kiss with soft lips on her flesh. Her core pulsed at the thought.

"Hello... starving. We'll figure out the system and Anwar tomorrow. Tonight, we need to feed."

The older vampires grew, the less frequently they needed to feed. There were some specific schedules they needed to stick to, regardless. Farrah was much younger than Leila, so she would often need to go three to four times before Leila even got an inkling of hunger. Lately, though, Leila was feeding more and more, almost as if she were trying to fill some void. "Okay, feeders, or are we hunting?"

"I think hunting tonight."

No surprise there. Along with Leila's increased feedings, she almost never wanted the feeders anymore. "All right. Let's hit up the bikers down on Jefferson."

"I'll drive." Leila held up keys to her Hellcat. She was quite the speeder, and thankfully, she was able to glamour police officers, otherwise, she would have never gotten out of her many traffic violations.

"I know..." Farrah groaned. But she didn't put up a fight. Maybe Leila needed all her distractions. The hunting, the speeding. Even her alcohol intake was up. Whatever had happened with Mael, she seemed bound and determined to take it out on herself.

The sounds pumping from the speakers could be heard for miles around. It was a typical night of drag racing and debauchery. In other words, an amazing night for vampires. Everyone in the immediate vicinity was either drunk or high. The most perfect conditions for hunting humans.

The areas near the track were thick with smoke from burning rubber and exhaust spilling from old-school cars. Despite not being a driver like Leila, Farrah still felt the thrum of excitement. It was a direct effect of hyped humans and plenty of hearts pulsing. Some of them even beat in time to the treble of hip-hop blaring in the streets. It was an extremely sexy scene, and if Farrah were like the others, she would have enjoyed it more.

"Leila, what's up, mamma?" A slightly hoarse voice came from behind them as they made their way across the parking lot.

They both turned around to find Frances—or Frank, as his friends called him. As one of the most dangerous vampires in Detroit, it was never good for him to catch another vampire on his turf. His turf was for those he'd turned and their guests. Without a personal invite, the interloper was as good as dead. Thankfully, Leila had leeway with him. She'd done him favors in the past, and he liked her bar. A good thing too, since he'd turned so many newbies he could run Detroit. If, and only if, he weren't so intimidated by the power the Order held.

"Frank. It's good to see you."

As he approached, he threw an arm around both of them, pulling them into a Black-and-Mild-scented embrace. "Better now that y'all are here." He released them after a few moments. "I was coming to see you, Leila. I can't find her. You have any luck the other day?"

Leila cocked her head and looked at him. He was obviously referring to Izzy. This was her scene, and whether she wanted anyone to know or not, Frank was her favorite entanglement.

"You know I'm talking about Izzy. I mean, I know we had an argument, but she ain't never been one to stay away for this long, know what I'm saying?" He clapped his hands together and rubbed them against one another. It was most likely an effort to look nonchalant. It wasn't working. Not even in the slightest.

"When's the last time you saw her?" Farrah interjected because Leila wasn't one to offer up anyone else's business. Was it possible the missing clients were related to Izzy's untimely disappearance?

"You know, I don't keep track... We gave each other some top one night, and she got pissed because I had plans for the night. Stormed off. I been calling and she ain't answering." Frank was an ominous creature, one who wasn't prone to hysterics or emotion, period. There he was, though, giving off worried boyfriend vibes in front of his entire crew. While they were immediately near one another, vampires could hear a rat piss on cotton. In their world, it wasn't prudent to show who they cared about because it could be used against them.

Leila was unmoved by his display, however. "I haven't

seen her. She'll turn up for you. Who could resist getting *top*, as you say, from you?" She walked away, but Farrah held back.

"Hey, what's your number? I'm looking for some friends too. I'll hit you up if I hear from her."

"Cool, that's what's up. Gimme your phone." A smile broke through his obsidian mask. He bit into his lower lip, obviously thrilled to have someone else on his team looking for Izzy.

Farrah handed him the phone, and he proceeded to punch in a number then hit the call button. A tone sounded out from one of his many pockets. "Okay, I'll give you a holler."

"Thanks. And um"—he looked around for a second —"since you did me a solid, I'm going to do you one. See that building over there?"

He pointed to the Harbor Town Towers in the distance.

"Yeah, what about 'em?"

"Hit it to the penthouse. There's a little feeding soiree going on up there, you heard me?"

Farrah caught his drift, and if she had bothered to feed earlier, she never would have taken him up on it. Frank's crew wasn't exactly her cup of tea. But even as he said the words, her fangs threatened to release. "Thanks, Frank."

"Knight..."

"Huh?"

"Around here, the humans call me Knight. C'mon, even you ain't that goofy. Can't have people looking into the details of your death, right?" He looked at her, skepticism in his eyes.

"Right, right." Farrah had forgotten, nearly. Vampire

identities were to be protected at all costs. Since she didn't mingle in clans, introvert that she was, she didn't have to take such pains to conceal who she was. She stuck to her own kind. Humans had a history of destroying anything they didn't understand. It was where all the lore came from. Once upon a time, there were hunters. It had taken centuries to erase true stories with smoke and mirrors. "Got it, Knight. I'm going to take you up on that offer. I just need to find Leila."

"Cool," he said, extending a hand. When Farrah took what was proffered, he enveloped her in a bone-crushing embrace, then released her. "So, when you get there, tell the doorman you're there for the Knight event. Take the elevator to the twentieth floor. We have the entire suite. Knock twice. They'll let you in. Bet."

"Thanks. See you over there."

"Yup yup." Then he was gone. His crew had been waiting a few hundred feet away. They encircled him as he approached.

Something was up, Farrah thought. Somehow, all the disappearances had to mean something. Since no one else seemed to be putting it together, it would be up to her to figure it out. Even if she didn't fully know what she was looking for.

# CHAPTER TEN

*A*tlanteans could live feeding once a month, given their age. But they did need to burn off steam. It was how he'd ended up at Knight's weekly bloodbath of a party. The humans were pre-sedated, thanks to a healthy dose of vampire venom. The only rules were to refrain from draining anyone. From what Anwar had heard, there were very few instances of such a thing coming to pass, even though there were no less than fifty vampires in attendance.

The taste of the female's blood on his tongue did nothing to mollify his hunger, though. She was a human, weak in comparison to Farrah, and her flesh was sagging around the neck from too many years of feeding. It was probably time for her to be retired. It was most likely the feeling of being fed from... like a gentle tug and kiss from inside, then hovering on the brink of orgasm until the vampire released. Orgasms were sure to follow. Some vampires had sex with their feeders since the scent of arousal was almost contagious. Anwar prayed Farrah wasn't one of those vamps.

He licked the feeder's wounds closed and released her from his hold. She flashed her blue eyes in his direction, probably with one thing on her mind from the smell of her. Anwar simply smiled, pulled a hundred from his pocket, and pressed it into her hand.

The brunette looked down at the bill, then back at Anwar with a big smile. Money meant so much to humans. "Thank you, Mr..."

"Tsedek. But please, I don't normally take a vein. Just accept this token and my apologies for being so... abrupt." Anwar layered charm into his stare to ease the human's anxiety. He'd been doing it as he drank from her, and now that she was looking at him, he wanted to be sure she wasn't experiencing any shock. He'd seen that before in feeders and could not bear to have it happen at his hand. They wouldn't remember what happened to them once the party was over, but it didn't mean he had to be inhumane. He'd never been human, but he knew its importance.

"Sure, sweetie. I didn't mind. Not even a little bit," she said. With a wink, she turned and left.

Anwar was glad when she strode from the room. She most likely needed to get herself a vegetable smoothie to help build her iron, given the amount he'd taken. They made them in the kitchen for the feeders. It didn't take long for his attention to shift back to Farrah. Even though she wasn't around him, he could swear he'd scented her.

He didn't want to think of her, but something about her made his heart race. She drove him to anxiety over what he would say when he next saw her. Something like, *hey, wanna kick it?* Wasn't that too nineteen-eighties? Anwar had never needed to woo anyone. While it sounded like bragging, it was true. Since Atlanteans served as the genesis of all vampires, they automatically submitted to him. Males and females. They had no idea of the reason, nor that it was biological. It just happened. The slightest suggestion an Atlantean made to a vampire was simply obeyed. It was the reason the Atlanteans' identities had been concealed by the Order to the masses. Atlanteans were as powerful as gods.

In most instances, his origin story would have been to his advantage. In this case, it sucked balls. To say his romance game was weak was right on the money. Somehow, though, he wanted to work on it... for her. She made him want to chase her. Not in the predatory way, either. When had it happened? Perhaps the day she'd helped him with his profile? When she laughed, it made his breath catch.

Whenever it was, he'd been thinking of her more and more.

The deeper he slipped into his thoughts of her, the greater his longing. A low growl emitted from his chest as he imagined her eyes on his as he suckled a cherry. Ridiculous. That was exactly what he was being. He stalked from the room, frustrated by his infatuation with a female who didn't seem to be concerned with him at all. Perhaps she desired him, but was that even what he wanted? He seemed to consider things other than her beauty. She was indeed gorgeous, a pint-sized delicacy. She was also smart, and... friendly. Something he didn't think he'd ever seen in a female vampire. Even the Atlanteans had been curt and cold.

Oh yeah. He was gone.

As he walked from one of the back rooms, the scent of rhododendrons and lilacs flooded the air, their soft notes evocative in the evening breeze. The fragrance of the summer flowers was all-consuming for a moment. He'd had the pleasure before and knew it could only be one female. Farrah filled his senses. Either he was going insane, or she was somewhere in that penthouse.

There were a few more people there since he'd been in the room with the feeder. As he searched for Farrah, he wanted to pick everyone up in his path and throw them. He was dominant to every being in the room and while they instinctually parted as he approached, it wasn't fast enough.

He made his way into what should have been a formal dining room. Instead, it was littered with loveseats and lounge chairs, each occupied with a coupling: a human and a vampire. For feedings that would not require the subcomponent of sex, they took care of their blood needs in the open. Searching the den, he saw a glorious crown of black curls splayed over the chest of a man. The scent of her grew stronger, and he knew, even without seeing her face, it was *his* Farrah.

Without regard for who he was stomping over, he practically dove across the room and grabbed her arm. The result was yanking her off the young human, a stream of blood landing artistically on the pair of lips emblazoned on her T-shirt.

"What the fuck," she exclaimed, one hand going to her mouth to catch the blood.

Anwar didn't know what to say to her. The primitive parts of him roared to life and without even a second glance at the dazed and confused human, he stormed off, dragging Farrah behind him.

"Let me go, Anwar. I was feeding. In case you're wondering, it's called nutrition for a reason. I'm going back," she yelled at him as he skillfully maneuvered the crowd.

Like hell she would. Anwar surprised himself by not saying it aloud. But that was the end of the surprises. Without another word, he grabbed her hand and strode through the rooms until he found one unoccupied. After hauling her inside, he turned and closed, then locked the door. The moment he was done, the ice-cold sting of a slap met his jaw.

"How fucking dare you to drag me down a hallway like some kind of caveman? I am a fully grown-ass female, and I'm sorry, but in the last decade or so, alpha has been out. That includes vampires." She was seething based on the immediate chill in the air around him and the hyper-extended fangs. Her arms were crossed over her chest, but even with that, he could see her lengthened nails.

Anwar had never been slapped before. As with most things Farrah did, it was a new experience. "I'm sorry, I—"

"I... I... Fuck that. You cannot drag me around like that. I'm not your female. And I'm not sure whether you know what consent is or not, but we are in a room alone. Unless that's an eggplant in your pants, you thought we were going to... to what, exactly, Anwar?"

He didn't even need to look down to know his cock was on display. Slacks had been a bad idea, but then again, he was supposed to be on a date that evening. "I wasn't going to force myself on you," he said, holding both hands over his dick.

"Really, then what was the plan?" She glanced around the room and waved her hand in the direction of the four-poster bed in the center. "We were going to work on your profile again? Maybe do some needlepoint?"

"No," he said, agitation adding punctuation to his words. "I didn't want you feeding from that... human."

"Really? That's the best you can do? In case you're wondering, it's what we do."

"I want you to feed from me." His voice was foreign, even to his own ears. A guttural command bubbling forth as if from a caged beast deep inside him, daring to take control.

And, for the first time since he'd seen her that evening, no words were coming out. Opening her mouth, she started to say something then obviously thought better of it. She shut it, opened it once more, then shut it again. A long blink and head-shaking clued him in on the inevitable rejection.

"I don't want you to feed from anyone else, ever again." He added the clarifying statement in case she wasn't getting his point. Hell, even he wasn't getting it. He hadn't expected to be honest with her. It was useless, though. If he thought about it, he'd been infatuated with her from the moment Mael showed him her video for VMA.

"You do realize that would mean we'd be blood-mated, don't you?"

"Yes. I'm aware," he said, trying to keep the questioning out of his voice. Farrah did that to him. Utterly confounded his thoughts in a way no one had, ever.

"I... I didn't check to see if we were a match. I thought about it, but it wouldn't have been right." Her eyes were wide then, less angry.

"I think..." He couldn't believe the words forming in his mind. His hands clenched as he fought against a rising swell in his chest. "I think you're what I was looking for. Something I didn't know I needed."

Even as he released the words, fear crept into his soul. He knew what being blood-mated meant. And she didn't even know what he was. Only that he stood before her offering himself. The temptation to tell her would have to be abated. If she wasn't his mate, she could never know the truth. It all hinged on the next words from her delicious lips.

## CHAPTER ELEVEN

*W*hat the hell was he saying? Surely, Farrah thought, she hadn't heard his towering ass correctly. Was he picking the exact wrong moment to declare himself her mate? "I don't think you know what you're saying."

"I can assure you, before the words tumbled from my mouth, I considered them carefully."

"Now, there's romance right there."

He moved closer. "I'm interested in you, and perhaps mating is hasty..." Once he reached her, he bent over and captured her chin. "How about something more in line with your business? We can *date*?" Coming from him, dating sounded like some foreign concept.

Despite her initial objections, hearing his proclamation and request made her tighten deep inside, dangerously close to her core. "I could. I mean, we could, I guess or whatever." Clasping her hands together in an effort to stave off her fidgeting, she maintained eye contact, even though she wanted to break it.

"I guess we could or whatever? Who's the romantic one now?"

"So, what are we... what are we doing here?"

The ever-present intensity of his gaze softened for a moment, and in his eyes, she found warmth. Kindness. It was something she hadn't seen in vampires in all the time she'd been one. "I'm going to kiss you, Farrah. It will be the beginning of our courtship."

"Courtship? I don't think I did that even when I was human. How old are you, anyway?"

"A millennia. Now, if you could be quiet for just a moment, I should like to kiss you."

"To be clear, I'm not ready to simultaneously exchange blood, thus becoming your blooded mate. I need to know you're good with that." She hoped he could see the pleading in her eyes. She'd been taught that blooded mates were dangerous. Leila instilled it in her every chance she got. She wasn't about to drop the ball for some gorgeous, sex-on-a-stick vampire who'd come out of nowhere and slipped in through a blind spot. Looking at him, though, she knew it was probably going to be the last shred of self-preservation she would be able to hold on to.

"I don't believe I've ever had to work so hard for a kiss. It's new and... interesting. But, if it puts your nerves at ease, I'm not interested in mating immediately, either. Love at first bite sounds good and all, but it could prove disastrous. Now, what about this kiss I'm frankly pleading for right now?"

Anwar hovered, his mouth just over hers, so close she could smell his heavenly scent. The fall of his locs enveloped them, a cocoon of raw sexual energy. As close as he was, she could feel his hardness against her stomach, briefly imagining what he would feel like inside her. She nodded, giving him permission to claim her mouth, and whatever else he may have wanted from her.

He closed the distance, a kiss at first gentle, then deepening. His hands went around her body, resting on her ass and squeezing as he took her. Their kiss intensified, turning into something demanding and rough. Her fangs extended of their own volition and sank into the softness of his lip. He tasted sweet, like a strong wine of an ancient vineyard. She'd never had anything the likes of him and knew if she ever let him go, it would be eons before she did again.

"Farrah," he breathed. In one smooth movement, he lifted her, and she wrapped her legs around his waist.

She could feel his hardness pressing into the heated softness of her pussy. She wanted him inside her, and there was no way they would be able to stop themselves. She knew this fact as much as she knew her own name.

Breaking the connection, Anwar began walking them to the bed. "Since claiming a female is passé, how do you see this going?" His voice was a low-throttle growl.

Farrah tightened her grip around his neck and practically melted against him. "I think we should start out slowly." She licked her lips at the thought of him inside her. "No blood exchange yet. We'll alternate." The way her words scattered across her mind at his touch, she was surprised she could speak at all. But, if they did drink from one another simultaneously, the full impact of the blooded mating would occur. They would become dependent on one another.

"You may go first. Anything else?" Anwar reached the bed, and as he spoke to her, he gently laid her body down, holding eye contact.

"After tonight, we use our words. If you see me doing

something you dislike, we'll talk about it." Another proud moment, considering her lady parts were about to pulse out of her jeans.

Anwar grimaced. He stepped away and undid his belted slacks. "May I have a stipulation, please?"

"I guess so." Farrah sat upright and stripped the bloody T-shirt off, practically drooling when his trousers hit the floor. He was definitely well endowed.

"I don't want you to feed on anyone else during our courtship."

"Ballsy move. May I ask the same of you?"

Anwar smirked, the common expression somehow irresistible on him. "I hardly ever feed. That is no problem for me." He yanked his shirt open, the sound of buttons raining around the room.

"Fine then," she said, opening her own pants and sliding them down her legs. She was stripped to her undies and lingered as she got to the front clasp of her bra.

"What are you waiting for?" he asked, stepping out of Calvin Klein briefs.

"Just enjoying the show."

"Here"—his voice came out as if he were being choked—"have a closer look." In one fluid movement, he lunged for her. He stripped off his shirt, revealing a brilliantly intricate upper sleeve of tattoos. Once he was nearly on top of her, he ripped the lacy panties free and pulled at the straps of her bra when he was done.

Farrah squeezed her eyes shut from pleasure as he licked up her neck luxuriously. She struggled to focus as his mouth moved over her skin. Everything in her body craved him, an overwhelming hunger to revel in his touch. She needed him, her core aching for anything he would offer her. "Your tats..." She ran a finger over the swirling mass of markings prominently displayed on his shoulder and running down his forearm. "I've never seen anything like them."

He stopped his ministrations over her body and looked into her eyes. "They're kind of a family thing."

"I love them. Who's your artist?" Any grip she could manage on reality would keep her from being lost to him forever.

"You want to talk tattoos when I can do this?" With a sinister grin and flaming blue eyes, he leisurely lapped at her exposed nipple. As his gaze trained on her face, she trembled in his arms. She could feel the weight of his gaze against her skin, the heaviness of his visual caress laying her bare. He nipped at her, laved her taut nub with his tongue, which sent her back into a stiff arch as waves of pleasure washed through her, threatening to drive her over the edge.

Running her finger across the fine etchings in his flesh, she savored the feel of him. He was silky and smooth, a contrast with the corded muscles in the most delicious of ways. "You, Mr. Tsedek, may become my guilty pleasure," she said on a laugh.

"Oh, I'm betting on that." A warm, heated mouth trailed its way downward—between her breasts, over her stomach, and into the very center of her body.

A violent shudder ripped through her, sending her back into a high arch. Her legs fell open wide as she submitted herself to him. His hands squeezed her legs to near impossible angles as he laved his tongue over her clit, then into her canal. In a circular motion, he licked her top down and back again. "Anwar," she bit out, her hands sinking into luxe locs and pushing him deeper.

Without any regard to appearing depraved, dying of

thirst for him and his touch, she rode him on a wave of overwhelming ecstasy. Her thighs trembled against his tight grip, and he had no mercy on her as she whimpered and pleaded with him to stop. No, no, she craved his touch, desperate for him to keep filling her to the brim with his particular brand of torturously decadent delight.

She hungered for him, and on a surge of adrenaline, she clawed at him. Farrah was sure he could have overpowered her if he so chose. There was only one reason he wouldn't do that in the moment. It would have to be because he wanted her to be fully satisfied. "I need you inside me," she whimpered.

Hooded eyes stared back at her. Between the two of them was a heated connection neither of them could deny. Whatever it meant, and whatever may happen, she needed this, and she would revel in their union even if she knew what they were doing was probably a one-time thing. Anwar had *love them and leave them* written all over him.

But she didn't care. She wrapped her legs around him and drew him closer, hanging on to strong shoulders and settling her heels into his lower back. "I want you inside me," she demanded.

"And I will give you everything you need. But next time, it'll be my turn. Tomorrow night, we're going to the Tabernacle. It will be our first date. And I can't wait to show you off."

She wanted to tell him there wouldn't be a next time if he didn't meet her demands. The things she was asking didn't seem to fit his MO.

Before she could come up with any kind of sassy comeback, he latched on to her breast, starting again with his fingers deep inside her. This male could literally break her, but she could not wait for him to fill her to the brim with his sex inside hers.

"If you say so," she whispered through heavy panting. He was able to somehow make her forget everything, giving rise to a hunger of the most epic proportions.

Elegant fingers slid out of her and left a trail of fire behind them as he ran them into her hair. Something about their connected gaze reminded her of Leila's warning—he would be a hard male to get over. But did she care?

In a controlled stroke, something that felt as if it were meant to drive her insane, he pressed inside her, his cock filling each inch of her sex. "Oh, Anw—" His name died on her tongue as he moved inside her. The only thing she could manage was a strangled demand. "Deeper."

The reply was a powerful thrust that made the bed squeak over the wooden floor. "I have no problem with that." Anwar's hips rolled against her as if to punctuate her demand. He licked up her neck, then, with measured intensity, he took her away on a wave of sensuality.

She did not know how to keep herself grounded, to stave off the urge to offer him everything she had to give. And with one more intense, gratifying stroke, she lost the will to care.

## CHAPTER TWELVE

*MAEL*

Mael sat on the only available park bench, watching over the most important thing in his long life—Lani. The playground was filled with children playing with other kids and distracted parents on their mobile phones.

Just beyond them was a food truck that sold baked goods. The smells of cinnamon rolls and sticky-sweet pastries wafted on the summer breeze. The picturesque day should have been what humans would have called perfect. Yet, it was far from it.

Lani was on her second awakening. Every fifty years, she would wake up with her memory gone in a new place. Mael hated the process. But since she didn't age past her fiftieth year, it was the only way. The labor was hell, and the pay was even worse. But it had been Azazel's dying wish. And if Mael was anything, he was loyal to his angel brethren. Even though all of them had turned their backs to him. One day, he would need to reconcile with all those he'd wronged.

His loyalty to his kind had been the reason he'd left Leila. A female like that he would never be able to lie to. To protect the Nephilim meant keeping her a secret. Even from those Mael loved the most. Besides, if the archangels found out Lani was exhibiting powers, anyone who knew would be executed. Leila didn't deserve that.

When his phone vibrated in his pocket, he knew it was going to go from bad to worse. "Make it quick," he barked into the receiver, drawing attention from a nearby mom who was gently pushing the stroller in front of her back and forth. He waved and nodded in understanding, which at least made her take her dagger eyes off him.

"Don't be testy, Maelstrom," Viktoria said. "I think you're aware we're looking for weekly status reports. And unless some catastrophic event wiped out all the cell phone towers, I haven't received your call."

"I'm working on it."

"So, no good news. Is he any closer to the female?"

"No, not yet. He's not mated."

"How can you be sure?" Viktoria's voice was spiked with venom and distrust.

"Well, I think you know angels can sense the duality of souls. He was not mated last I saw him."

"We don't have all year, Mael. Get a move on. Otherwise, I'll be forced to play the cards I've been dealt. We need to get rid of the Atlanteans before Constantine awakens." The part she left unsaid was the threat they proved to be for Viktoria. As a vampire, Viktoria's true nemeses were Atlanteans. Naturally stronger, and if they were to decide one day to seize power, there was nothing to stop them. Getting rid of them would leave the crux of power to vampires since they outnumbered most of the more powerful races and were stronger than the remainder in brute strength. She wanted control. Absolution. Ultimately, she wanted to enforce changes the Atlanteans opposed. And they had the ability to end her without even touching her. She knew it. Anwar and Constantine knew. And a violation of the accords was the only way to be rid of them permanently.

Mael closed his eyes, leaning back on the bench. He was beyond tired of being threatened. Of having his family threatened. Though Lani wasn't his blooded daughter, she was his charge. "Are you responsible for the missing females?"

There was silence on the other end for a beat. Long enough to make him check the phone to see if that call was still connected. "How did you know about that?"

"Anwar. He mentioned when he arrived home last evening some females have gone missing."

More silence. Finally, he heard her clear her throat. "I don't know of any missing females. Their races would have brought them up to the Order, surely. That's beside the fact. Just get Anwar together. I'll speak to you again soon."

That time the call did end, and he shoved the phone back into his pocket. Besides the power grab, Mael had other suspicions too. He wouldn't put it past the Order to take the females for whatever diabolical game they were playing. While he hadn't been privy to the full details, there were things he had overheard. Something to do with gene splicing. Atlantean genes, but that was all he'd made out. The Order members present had stopped speaking when they saw him enter the room.

She'd seemed stunned, not guilty, but that didn't

mean anything. And while she had him by his balls, he would not allow any harm to befall the humans. And he would figure a way out of his situation.

Then... perhaps, he would deal with his situation with Leila. Seeing her again had set his soul on fire. Every time he thought of her, his cock grew as hard as Enochian steel. Every image of her in his mind made him want to fuck her senseless. With each passing year, the cracks in his heart deepened. His longing like an albatross that dragged him further and further into the depths of loneliness. Even if they could never be in another relationship, he would make her understand. It had been so many years ago, but their life together had been crystal clear. Had he not been called away to help Azazel, he would have stayed with her. And maybe, just maybe, he wouldn't be in the position he was currently faced with. Maybe, it would have been forever.

As they said, however, hindsight was always twenty-twenty.

## CHAPTER THIRTEEN

*A*nwar had kept Farrah awake since they'd parted at dawn. She tossed and turned all day, analyzing every single word he'd said the night before. Even worse, she'd been analyzing every word he hadn't said, because what the hell did that mean?

She rolled over, not wanting to answer the phone as it interrupted her obsessing. She picked it up and didn't even have to glance at the screen to know who it was. "Evening, sunshine." Leila's voice burst onto the line. "You're still in bed?"

The initial mental response to this would have made Leila hang up on her. Instead, she replied, "I'm fully aware."

"Are you staying in bed all night? Or can you walk today?"

The question let her know Leila had seen her with Anwar. And since they'd stayed in that random bed nearly until the sun rose, she probably was fully aware of the goings-on. "He asked me on a date."

"Wow. So, what is this? Boyfriend girlfriend, or just fuck buddies?"

"I don't know yet. We're *courting*."

"Courting? Hmph. He didn't seem like the type."

"Yeah, I know. Tonight, after work, he's taking me to the Tabernacle."

"Uh-huh. Well, then. Get up. We're gonna eat and then go shopping. The stores will close in three hours. Stop playin' and handle your scandal." The clapping sound coming through the receiver had to be her hands slapping together in rapid, exceedingly annoying, succession.

Farrah wasn't exactly the early-nightfall type of female. She normally didn't rise until the sun had been down an hour or so. She also hadn't shared her promise to Anwar that they wouldn't feed from anyone else. It was one she wanted to keep, but not something she could tell Leila. She was anti-relationship and would not understand such loyalty to someone who hadn't even crossed the mating threshold.

"Blah," she croaked into the receiver while simultaneously taking the pillow off her head. "Maybe we could skip the shopping and I could wear something I have... or something of yours." She winced at this. Leila wasn't exactly into sharing her clothes. There was no fashionista honor in that.

"Something you have? You dress with that stoner-girl grunge chic. You know what that is? It's deceased fashion. Even when it was in, it was out. Like twenty years ago. There's a whole new name for what you are. You need to get fly. Otherwise, you'll never fit in at a place like the Tabernacle. I don't care what anyone says. A well-dressed woman is a force to be reckoned with. You can't be reckoned with in someone else's clothes. It's unseemly. Now go on. Get dressed. I'm coming over in a few minutes."

More with the squinting and procrastinating, but Farrah knew in her soul she'd lost already. "I just need one more hour," she pleaded, unsure of whether it was more sleep she was after or if it was just shopping avoidance. They both would fit the bill.

"Fine, I'm not bringing you food. You'll have to fend for yourself tonight. Lazy self."

Over the open phone line, she heard Leila rustling around and realized she would probably have about ten minutes before she flew over. The older the vampire, the faster they flew. Farrah was something like a person running. A really fast person. Like Usain Bolt. Leila was closer to a car on the freeway.

An older vampire could make it to Europe in a few hours. Useful, should the need arise to avoid the whole TSA circus. They just needed to level up before it could be done. From Leila's to Farrah's house? Farrah had seen Leila do it in under a few minutes.

"Get dressed. I'm on my way. You'll have a little extra time since I'm driving." The phone died before Farrah could get in a snide comment.

With an audible moan, she planted her feet on the plush carpet. She deplored the stuff. She was more of a hardwood girl. But try to find that in an apartment... Just made sense to leave the house thing alone. Daytime lawn-cutting was probably a no-go. Carpet was her cross to bear, then.

She took a hot shower to warm her blood and was standing in front of the mirror applying a coat of Carmex before Leila got there to berate her. And miracle of miracles, she made it to being dressed and on the couch with minutes to spare. Leila never bothered with the knocking thing, just barged in as usual, her movement from the patio into the apartment like flash photography.

Her face resonated with whatever she was thinking, hitting Farrah straight in the kisser. "Oh, I'm sorry. Did you shower? From the look of those clothes, you must have just gotten up."

Farrah was used to it. Fashion was Leila's love language. At times, it was a surprise she'd even turned her since she had never been one to hazard a second glance at someone like Farrah. Farrah had long since given up trying to understand why. Over the years, though, they'd become closer than most vampire/maker relationships. "Girl, one day you're gonna barge in here and I'll be using my bullet. It'll be the shock of a lifetime. I promise you, you don't wanna see it."

The quizzical look on Leila's face was followed by, "What's a bullet?"

It took Farrah a few seconds to recover from dissolving into laughter. "What do you mean?"

"A bullet. What is that?" The look on her face was earnest.

"It's like the thing you use to"—she motioned with her hands to her pelvic region to give Leila a clue—"to..."

"To jump rope?"

"Girl, it's a toy."

Shrugging, Leila gave her another flatline look.

"It's a sex toy." She waved her hands then, motioning for her what it would look like, sans small vibrating toy.

"Ugh..." Leila twisted her face, feigning disgust.

"You never... Never mind. Somehow, I feel like this is a conversation for folks who actually have a sex drive and no boo thing."

Shaking her head, Leila pulled a bag from somewhere behind her. "Whatevs. Here..." She tossed the bag with precision aim. Farrah caught it and opened it. Inside was a designer pair of jeans, a billowy shirt in charcoal gray, and some slate gray stilettos because yeah, that's what people do. "Put those on. Otherwise, where we're going shopping, they'll think you're a homeless person and won't serve you."

"I thought a woman couldn't be reckoned with in someone else's clothes?"

"Don't be a smartass." Leila pointed at Farrah, then aggressively at the clothes. "Those aren't mine. I always have spares for you in case of a fashion emergency."

With a sigh, Farrah rolled her eyes. "I don't wanna shop at some pretentious-ass spot with a bunch of assholes. I'll end up on the news for draining one of 'em. And where the hell did you pull these from? Do you just walk around with fly-ass clothes at the ready?"

"You don't need to know my secrets. Now, c'mon. You know you're too much of a softy to drain a human. And here, stop wearing that Dollar Haven lipstick. Put this on," she said, leaning forward and pressing a tube of MAC Velvet Teddy lipstick and Chestnut lip liner into Farrah's hands. "Even the natural look takes a little work, sweetie."

With that, she turned and headed into the kitchen, leaving Farrah standing there with a handful of clothes she would have never even known where to buy they were so expensive.

If she didn't love her dearest friend so much, she would have staked her ass right in the heart. Despite all the snark and bossiness, Farrah knew Leila wanted what was best for her. Even if Leila wasn't into the whole mating scene, she would not stand in Farrah's way. That was what this whole shopping thing was. An attempt to get the finest for Farrah. And that was the reason Farrah headed into the bathroom with the clothes.

After changing into the fancy clothes, putting on the goddamn lipstick, and fluffing her hair with glossing spray, she did truly see a difference. Twirling in the mirror a couple of times, she had to admit Leila was right. She looked good, much to her chagrin. She hated when Leila was right, which was pretty fucking often.

"Okay, you damn bully. Come and see your work," she called out. Taking another spin, she tried to find something—anything—wrong so she could point it out. But there was nothing. She also was enjoying the way the cut of the blouse and jeans fit, accenting her curves. "I could just wear this on the date."

Within seconds, Leila was standing in the doorway with a condescending grin playing on her lips. "See... look at that shit. It's awesome. Amazing. Flawless." She clapped her hands, pressing her fingers to her lips as if she were staring at an original Picasso. "But no, this isn't Tabernacle-worthy. You need something else. Come now, the mall's closing soon."

"I still say I'm overdone for shopping. My feet are gonna ache the whole time." The stilettos were cut low on the toe and pointy. Probably cost a fortune too.

"Your feet shouldn't hurt from two hours of heels. You wear cheap shoes. These are Christian Louboutin. They won't fucking hurt. Now, c'mon. I'm starved," Leila said with a roll of her eyes and flipping her pristine hair over her shoulder. The blunt ends overlapped themselves the way precision cuts did.

Farrah mimicked her silently before shutting the lights off and following her out of the bathroom. "Fine," she said. "Oh, I need one second. I'm going to have Ennis start looking into the app to see if he can dig up any more information about the missing clients." Farrah took her wallet from the kitchen counter and headed toward the door to her apartment.

"Well, you know how Ennis loves to sleuth. Give the male what he wants."

"Indeed." After grabbing her cell and keys, she tapped the text out telling him what happened and what she needed. To which he replied, "*K.*" In Ennis's case, it meant he was on it. It was the thing she most appreciated about her tech guru—his willingness to work all night for her.

After Leila stepped into the hallway, Farrah followed and locked the door before they boarded the elevator, then made it across the lobby in record time. Their haste didn't stop the eyes of every human they passed from watching their every move. Farrah walked through that lobby every day and had never gotten so many head-turns and lingering glances.

They climbed into Leila's car and took off. For the entirety of the trip, Farrah worked on trying not to notice her lack of vampy ways and feeling somehow less than. In the beginning, she'd thought it would get easier. Maybe she would pick up on some things, others would come over time. So far, though, not much had changed between her days as a human and now. And she would be lying if she said it hadn't bothered her.

Leila had selected Somers Mall, which held some of the swankiest department stores that Michigan had to offer. Farrah felt bougie the moment she walked through the frameless glass doors and was immediately out of place. Her norm was the Gap or some other store with nondescript attire. She bought most of her graphic tees from ads on social media. Leila's mission was to make sure that Farrah was made over into something someone could love... or any ol' body could love. She carried on like a trooper and sat down as Leila went to find one of the salespeople in Neiman Marcus.

Fingering the material of one of the fancy dresses closest to her seat, she almost felt bad for touching it. They just *felt* different than clothes from the lower-end shops she frequented. Perhaps this would be like one of those movies where the nerdy girl whipped off her glasses and realized she was actually Lindsay Lohan. Though she knew she was no Lindsay.

"Here we are," Leila chimed as she came back around the corner with some pretentious-looking woman in dark suiting that most likely had some fancy color name. Something like weathered gray or silver mist.

"Hello, my dear. Oh, my goodness... What we have here?" she questioned with the affected accent of a one-percenter.

Already, Farrah knew exactly what she meant by her query. "I'm here under duress, so be easy on me," she said. She really wanted to tell her if she fucked with her, she would drain her dry, which was a lie. She would never drain anybody. But she would drink enough to make a bitch woozy. Her fangs itched to sink into the woman's neck.

Farrah turned and shot eye daggers in Leila's direction.

"Yes, well..." the woman said, dissatisfaction dripping from her voice. "We'll try and do something for you, but what are you going to do with your hair?"

Farrah immediately ran her fingers through her hair, disrupting her curly locks. "I'm not doing anything with my hair," she said. There was a fine line between being polite and being an asshole.

"Okay, suit yourself," the woman said, walking away only to return a few moments later with bolts of clothing. They looked amazing—everything from casual to fine dining to evening gowns. It was an array worthy of a princess. "No, no," she said when Farrah reached for one of the soft cotton blouses. "Let's do the evening gowns first. We have to get you fitted into some foundational garments to hold all your... stuff together."

She waved her hands around in the air as she gestured at what she must have considered Farrah's *stuff*. In a flash, she was out of there like a superhero trying to right some terrible injustice.

She must have been a gold medalist in the retail Olympics, because before Farrah could turn and curse Leila out—who sat in the corner smirking and completely enjoying her all kinds of discomfort—the woman was back, her arms loaded with ultra-constricting, body-reshaping underwear. Like torture garments that had no reason to ever be created.

Farrah walked into the dressing room that was already open, then dropped the clothes on the bench inside. As she closed the door, quick footsteps returned with more items. All of it very, very suspect micro material and fabric. After she tried to put on the extreme restriction garment that must've been used as a straitjacket, she heard Leila and the little woman giggling and laughing like they were planning her demise. Paranoid much? Instead of being neurotic, Farrah focused on getting her rolls into the sausage casing that doubled as Spanx. And struggled. Then she struggled some more.

The Lycra material popped, snapped, and smoothed into place, finally. In what she could only describe as a breath-confining nightmare, she could barely breathe and shit was riding up. In all the wrong places.

The dark blue, sparkly material glimmered under the fluorescent lighting. The train was a material akin to chainmail and fell three inches over the floor. Sliding the silky garment over her head, she pulled the dress down, hoping like hell she didn't rip the thing to shreds. Once she slid the spaghetti straps into place and closed the side zipper, she ran a hand over the smooth fabric. Perhaps there was more to this clothes thing than she allowed herself to believe.

As she turned, she could see parts of it were opaque, offering daring peeks at her flesh in strategically placed geometric patterns all over. She was pretty curvy, and most designers avoided that shit like the plague. It was a high-low cut number, and it fell in all the right places over her curves, designed to accentuate her bust line. Reviewing herself in the mirror, she was... Damn. Hot damn. If Anwar truly did think she was hot before, wait until he saw her in that thing. With a spin, she looked at herself from all angles and wondered how she'd never noticed the importance of a body shaper... Hell, maybe she did need to deal with her curls. Nah. F that.

"Leila, can you come in, please?" she called out to the waiting area.

"Yeah," Leila said, arriving too quickly at the door in front of a human. Leila wasn't exactly one to follow protocol, however.

Opening the door slowly, Farrah stepped out a bit and waited for a reaction. "What do you think?" She still had part of her body inside the room like an escape route. The dress went up at her knees and dropped low onto her calves. The top was loose-fitting yet looked tailored. It was a first-date type of dress. If she bent over, you could see the tops of her breasts, giving it a peekaboo-type sex appeal.

"Girl, you have to buy that one."

Farrah smiled, knowing that Leila was the type of friend who would tell the truth about what you looked like. None of that spare-your-feelings stuff that seemed shortsighted and at times intentional. She was a road dog, for real.

"So, every color of this one?" she asked, not really sure.

"Yup. Except yellow. It makes you look like Bananas in Pajamas. What's next?"

"I've got some more cocktail and then a couple of formal ones. Then we can do casual... apparently. Why the hell are you asking me anyway? You and Madame Chanel are driving this bus."

"Uh-uh. That's where you're wrong," said her friend. Leila shook her head in what must have been an effort to drive home the point. "We're here for you. Do your thing. We'll find you the perfect look for this jagoff Anwar. He's truly up to something, you know."

Farrah could have hugged her. She could see that

Leila was trying her best not to make her uncomfortable. Not that she could help it. She was just blunt. Farrah had learned to deal with it long ago. "I know, Leila. He could be. But sometimes"—she started, letting the door go and closing herself back into the tiny dressing room—"you have to take chances in order to see what life has to offer. Besides, we have a lot longer to get over heartache than most."

Farrah heard the guffaw on the other side of the door. "Ahhh, whatevs. Move on to the next dress, Farrah. We only have an hour or two. And we still need to eat."

Farrah knew what Leila was hinting at and dreaded it.

By the time she was done, she looked more and more like a member of elite vampire society. She totes wasn't. Like, she wasn't even in the middle class. She and Leila rarely even fraternized with their culture, so how could they be high society? Normally, she didn't care. It was just that she had no idea what Anwar was. If they did—big-ass *if*—if they did start dating, she wouldn't know how to present herself to his bigshot friends.

Well, the old saying, *better to arrive late than ugly*, would probably play into the situation a lot if dating were even on the table. Sure, he was taking her out, but she still needed to guard herself. She knew his type.

The next dress was even more of a sure thing. It was a cherry red formal gown with a sweetheart neckline. Farrah looked like a million bucks, at least she felt like she did when she stepped out again. With a glance over to Leila, who was now sitting on the couch with a bunch of other dresses thrown on top of her lap and the bougie retail lady, Farrah caught both of their reactions to the dress. It was evident that it was a keeper. She'd never seen anyone look at her as if she were the best-dressed thing in the room before.

She turned to the full-length mirrors that gave her three angles of shit. Now, that gave a different perspective. She was no longer completely confident.

"That's nice," Leila finally said.

"I guess..." Farrah said, trying to sound noncommittal and disinterested. Because you know, she put on thousand-dollar evening gowns every day. Oh yeah, because she was a fashion plate like that.

Farrah's cell phone ringing caught her in time to save Leila from her bitchy avoidance. "Can you hand me that?" Farrah asked her.

Leila picked it up and looked at the screen, then made a googly-eyed face. "I think it's him."

"It's who?"

"Annnwaarr," she said, juggling the phone as she walked toward Farrah.

"It's not," Farrah yelped, and snatched the device from her hands. She looked at the number and noted the foreign, yet familiar prefix. She hit the answer button quickly. Probably too quick. "Hello," she said, turning and walking away from the two women. The dress dragged on her sock-covered feet, and she nearly tripped over the yards of material.

"Farrah," he said, breathy and hot into the phone.

"Anwar, hi..."

"Are you... busy?" he asked. His voice was curious, not the same tone he'd had the night before.

"I'm not exactly busy. I'm out shopping with Leila... Picking up new clothes. It's been forever since I've done that, you know? I'm surprised I knew my sizes anymore. I buy most of my clothes from Amazon." The laugh she let off was awkward and silly, similar to a teenager's. *Shut up, Farrah,* she chided herself for rambling. She rolled her eyes skyward, thankful they hadn't Facetimed.

"I see. Well, I just wanted to make sure we were still on for tonight. At nine thirty, yes?"

Farrah turned to face Leila, mouthing the words *he's confirming for tonight.* They were like teens freaking out over a prom date. Farrah knew Leila was most happy about her getting some and not the possibility of a blooded mate. She wasn't anti-sex, after all. "Absolutely... I should be back home by then," she said, pointing to Leila's watch. Leila nodded, a sly smile on her lips.

"Great. I should ask, though. Have you ever been to the Tabernacle? I mean, it's not like Leila's bar. I just don't want you to be uncomfortable." Based on the tone of his voice, he seemed genuinely concerned.

"I don't normally go to underground vampire clubs, but I'm down to try new things," she said. Leila nudged her, shaking her head in a way that clued her in to having said something wrong. "I'm looking forward to it."

The laugh that came through the line let her know she probably had said something indicative of her general clueless nature when it came to flirting. The computer did the work at VMA. Farrah, on the other hand, strug-gled with in-person dynamics. Vampire social cues and the like. She was proving out the theory through her efforts with Anwar despite her best attempts.

"Okay, cool. And don't forget to text me your address. See you soon, my little vixen." His voice was a sensual growl coming through the receiver. It made her heat in low places.

As the line went dead, flashes of their sexual encounter went through her mind. If just his voice was doing that to her, how would she manage later? She also thought of other things... like her promise not to feed. Dammit... She took the phone off her ear and stared at it for a moment until a tap on the shoulder brought her back to the present. "Ow. Girl, what is—"

"First, you know I can hear what he's saying so no need to translate. Second, don't tell him you're down to try new things. We're vampires. You'll end up in Amsterdam snorting coke off the belly of some random pop singer. That leaves the door wide open to anything. You're a bit too tame to go down that path without a wing-person."

All Farrah could do was roll her eyes since some of her most depraved days had been spent with Leila. "Well... which pop star, because—"

"Uh-uh. Don't do that. You would freak the hell out, and don't pretend you wouldn't."

"Most likely," Farrah admitted, slipping back into the dressing room to change.

Once she was done, she came out and walked over to the sales lady, Crystal, according to her nameplate, who was pretending to ignore their conversation, and told her, "Give me the last two dresses and a couple of the jeans."

"Right away. I still think you should consider the salon to give you a nice sleek look." She smiled at Farrah, her full red lips unnaturally glossy.

"No, thank you. I'm good on the hair suggestion," she said, with more of a snap than a smile. The suggestion, Farrah knew, was a slap, a dig at her naturally curly hair, something all too common in the human world. Her fangs extended, completely outside of her control.

The lady jumped backward, her eyes wide with fear

at the sight of Farrah's fangs. Leila, who could always sense tension, was behind her in a millisecond.

Stepping around her, Leila stared into the eyes of the terrified woman, easing her fears with a mental grab at her cerebral cortex. "Tell her that her hair is gorgeous," Leila said.

"Your hair is lovely, really," Crystal said, voice still shaking despite the mind control.

"Thank you," Farrah said, grabbing her by the hand and pulling her forward. When they made it into the fitting area, Leila latched the door behind them.

Leila stepped closer, moving her hair over and revealing the curve of her neck and fingering the exposed skin before catching to woman's dilated gaze in the mirror.

"What do you think, Leila? Should we leave her memories or take them along with us?" Farrah sang.

"Leave her a couple. Just so she knows not to taunt the curly girls." Leila laughed as the woman sat on the bench, just as she'd been mentally directed.

"Sometimes, we should leave well enough alone, you know?"

"I do. C'mon. Let's not play with our food." Leila laughed again, her Southern drawl coming out stronger than ever.

Thankfully, Leila was preoccupied, so she didn't notice Farrah place Crystal's wrist in her mouth with no fang. She closed her lips over the site, careful not to puncture the skin. She faked with Leila to keep her promise to Anwar. He felt like a male she could trust. At least, she wanted to find out whether she could trust him. A wave of guilt washed over her, and Farrah told herself she would tell Leila everything later. When she knew for sure Anwar was someone who would be around for a while.

The resolution comforted her as she strategically allowed her hair to cover the *non*-bite. As she pondered what she thought of as betrayal to Leila, somehow it balanced out as she thought about whatever had happened with Mael. It must have been earthshattering for her not to tell Farrah about it. Hell, maybe turnabout was fair play?

"You look so tired, dear. Maybe you should head home for the night. Never fear, you've made quite the commission. You can afford to take a couple of days off." Leila nodded and the woman mimicked the motion of her head.

"Oh yes, I am a little tired, now that you mention it. I'll leave right after I restock these clothes. Have a wonderful day," Crystal said. "Good night, ladies."

With a wave, she stepped back into the bright fluorescent lights, and Farrah pretended to right herself, wiping at her mouth with the back of her hand. Leila was already ahead of her, as usual, and hadn't noticed Farrah's faux feeding.

"All right, let's go pay for this shit and get you dressed."

"You think I'll be overdressed?"

"I'm sorry, gonna take the fashion high road and say there's no such thing as too much. Besides, you look how you believe you look. And you must always believe that you're fierce. Then others will believe it, as well. The only thing you need is a little confidence."

"Yeah, no. I need a body double and a brain transplant. He is way outside of my level of hot. I'm a good five and a half. He's like a fifty, on a scale of one to ten," Farrah said.

Leila shook her head with a half-cocked smile. "C'mon. You're beautiful, best friend. You've got a date with a hot guy and bags of brand-new clothes. What's better than that?"

"Nothing," Farrah affirmed. But she actually wasn't sure. There was something just beneath the surface. Then again, there was more than she could account for in his eyes.

# CHAPTER FOURTEEN



The thought of Anwar's lie—rather omission of the truth from Farrah—crossed his mind. Omission, schmission. A lie was a lie. No matter what little game Anwar played, if she were to find out, she would no doubt be pissed. And he could very well lose the female.

Then again, who was Mael to talk about lies?

Back in the day, he wouldn't have even batted an eye. What had happened to careless Mael?

The question plagued him until he reached the front of the building and backed into the alley across from Farrah's apartment building. The newly gentrified community members would call it Martin Luther King Boulevard. But die-hard Detroiters knew what was up.

Once he was out of sight, he continued to beat up on himself for deceiving Anwar, and for giving a care about what he was doing. What kind of archangel did that? Have concern over friends and people he hardly knew?

Mael stepped out of the car when he could no longer stand being alone with himself. The flaps of the unseasonable leather jacket undulated on the wind, allowing cooler air to shoot in and chill his hind parts. Damn, Detroit was really taking that global warming thing to heart, with its rapidly changing weather.

Leila's car slid into a parking space. The inseparable pair stepped out with armloads of bags from some designer stores, and some nondescript with no logo or signage. Leila was still a big shopper, obviously. He used to love watching her get dressed. The meticulous way she chose every bracelet, shoe, bag, outfit, even the way she wore her hair to complement her chosen ensemble. As far as Mael was concerned, she could have worn a plastic garbage bag. She was beautiful no matter what she had on. Leila was happy, though. And that was the most important thing.

Farrah was pointing at her maker. Undoubtedly, they were cracking some kind of joke. Mael took an accounting of what Leila wore now that she was beneath the streetlights. She was elegant and graceful, just as he remembered. On anyone else, her clothes may have looked ordinary. But on her, she was a princess of the highest degree.

When he looked over at her, something in his gut told him he'd never stopped caring for her. It wasn't a lightning strike, not the fabled instant bond, and certainly not earth moving. It was knowing. And that firm knowledge took hold of him, grabbed his nerve endings, and snaked throughout his body. It was not one part of him that claimed her. It wasn't a heartache, or brain activity, or even in his manhood. All of him wanted to possess her and knew that someday he would.

In fact, his individual parts rallied. He watched as Farrah grabbed boxes and bags from the car and walked inside. His brain told him this was no good. Each time he thought of her, he felt his strength wane. A twinge in his muscles as if his power was passing through him.

There was a reason he had originally taken interest in her. Whether he knew what it was or not, he wanted to rip Viktoria apart for putting him in such a position. Much worse, he didn't appreciate having to play everyone who mattered to him. As much shit as he gave Anwar, he had kind of come to think of him as a friend. At least, the closest thing to constant that he'd had in the last century.

No, Mael was in deep shit. Farrah unlocked the door and went inside, Leila hot on her heels. When he could no longer see Leila, all of him—muscles, bone, and brain—ached longingly.

Oh yeah, he was wholly screwed. By the time it was all said and done, he would have betrayed everyone to save someone who didn't know he existed.

Fishing the phone from his pocket, he pulled up his texts with Viktoria. Tapping out the words, he knew there was no going back. *I'm in position. I'll let you know if he shows...*

CHAPTER FIFTEEN

There had been females throughout history who were said to have stripped males, hell, *kings*, of their ability to function with one fleeting glance. Their beauty and chemical attraction enough to stop the hands of time completely. But when Anwar had walked in to find her in that goddamned blue dress, he knew everything he'd felt was true and right.

Until that very moment, Anwar had called bullshit on all of it. Could you love, or even have an emotional connection, to someone you'd only known the sum total of a few hours? Not anymore. No siree, as the cowboy Americans said in those old-ass movies. Then, she opened the door of her apartment in a ridiculously ornate and beautiful ballgown-cut dress that made him want to tie her up with all the metal and switches and tricked-out accessories. She looked like a brand-new Harley. It was more than her look. It was the woman inside the clothes that had him wound up tight as a drum.

"Good evening," he said, attempting to control the panting.

"Hi, Anwar," she said. Her voice was warm, like hot chocolate. She stood to the side and let him come inside. With downcast eyes, she held on to the door and denied him a glimpse of her warm hazel eyes as he passed her. Through sheer luck, he brushed against her body then had to stabilize from the current that ran his length—both body and manhood.

"You did something different with your hair." But it wasn't the change at all. It was that it was away from her face, highlighting her elegant bone structure. And her eyes, her cheekbones, the planes of her face, stripped him of his breath. She was, if he only had one word to describe her, stunning.

As if self-conscious, she smoothed her hand over her flat-ironed hair. "Oh, I just um... wanted to try something different tonight."

He stood inside the dwelling, watching as she blinked, then turned and locked the door once again. He was happy she had bolted herself in. He knew all sorts of things bumped in the night just waiting to harm vamps. And that included the Order he was part of. He'd seen them do things on a whim, and while there was no reason for them to take an interest in Farrah, he still appreciated her being careful with her person.

"I'm not early, huh?" Anwar wondered if he'd managed to stabilize his voice.

She held a finger in the air, and a smile danced across her face. Goddamn if the heavens hadn't opened up and he'd seen the sun again. "Ahh, you are not. You, sir, are actually right on time. I just need to grab my little purse thing and we can go."

"Little purse thing. Okay," he said, turning to watch her as she passed. He was so damned uncoordinated around her that even his turn seemed to be jerky in movement.

"Yeah, it's little, little. Wait 'til you see it."

As she sashayed over, he surveyed the room in his old protective way. Seeing nothing out of the ordinary, he focused on the camera that was over the counter. She must have had some level of security in there, which made him feel better.

"Here it is," she said, back in his line of sight with a petite clutch shaped like an apple.

"Yup, it's a li'l thing, all right. I don't know why you're even carrying it. You could fit whatever you put in there in your pocket. Right?"

"Don't vampsplain me on purses," she said, popping him on his shoulder. "It's cute." With a laugh, she added, "And Leila said I have to carry one." As she rounded out her smile, he saw a difference in her in that moment. It was something he couldn't place, but she was not as happy as she had been earlier.

"Well, we can't let your maker down, can we? You look nice with it. Let's go. We're losing the night," he said, standing closer to her and touching her arm.

As she turned, he moved to her side and waited as she locked the door to her apartment. When she was done, he slid his hand to the small of her back, touching the place men longed for on women, and nearly knocked himself out from the impact. Memories of the prior night's activities flooded his mind. Contrary to popular belief, the most desirable place on a woman was the delicate curve of her spine just above the ass. At least, as far as he was concerned. Even as they moved from the building onto the street, he wanted to have her naked and pressed against his body. For now, he would settle for the gentle graze of her flesh through her skirt.

"I'm parked down here. I mentioned the Tabernacle, but I should reiterate. It's not like Frank's feeding brothels or Leila's clubs, although you'll see a few humans there."

"Yes, Leila warned me."

"And it's probably a bit wilder than you're used to."

"She warned me about that too," was all she said. Her voice was tiny on the walk to the car. She seemed thoughtful and reserved. She had been different the first day they'd met—hell, even earlier that morning when he'd left her. She'd giggled and been pleasingly aloof. This vamp before him was polished, yet nervous. He felt the anxiety rolling over her body in waves.

"And the first thing I want you to do," he said, grabbing her hand as he stepped into the street, "is relax. I am not here to judge you. You're a female who deserves the best. Let me help you get it." He looked both ways and walked in front of her, his hand firmly holding on to hers.

The train of her skirt scraped across the ground, heavy metal clinking with each step she took. Anwar had to hand it to her, however. She was certainly going to command attention. She looked like a battle maiden, ready for war. A medieval temptress, though she was hundreds of years too young for that.

Anwar hit the key fob to unlock his vintage Charger. When they were safely on the sidewalk again, he let her go. The headlights illuminated the dim alleyway, almond-shaped lamps lighting a path to his car. Farrah hadn't said a word. Instead, she walked to the passenger side and waited for him to open the door. When he reached her, he scented her. She smelled sweet and fertile, the hint of her essence spilling into the night air. He hadn't noticed earlier, but now it filled his nostrils and confounded his senses. He wanted her, but he needed to wait. To show her that he was decent. He didn't want to ruin his chances to be with her again. To one day tell her all the things he'd held back from her.

*Down boy*, he chided his inner beast. It scratched against the cage, rattling chains and hissing at the girl. Fuck yeah, he wanted her. Had she been any other female, he wouldn't have been so desperate. Somehow, Anwar didn't feel right about being *with* Farrah without being her blooded mate.

And where exactly in the fuck had that come from?

Grabbing her arm gently as if she were a doll made of the most delicate glass, he guided her into the passenger seat. When he released her, the feel of her soft skin was immediately missed. Ignoring the carnal urge of his *kensee* demanding he claim her, Anwar folded the chain-mail on the skirt and placed it in the car before he closed her in.

Honey-brown eyes, flitted with silver in the darkness, shined at him as if to ask why he was being so strange. He wouldn't be able to answer. Instead, he walked toward the back of the car, taking the long way around to the driver-side door. On the way, he shifted his tightening cock in his pants.

Fuck, that felt better. It was stiffening and trapped in the fitted pant leg. By the time he reached his car door, he was almost convinced he'd be able to comfortably sit down.

Deep inside, Anwar knew he should have called the whole thing off. He was going to fall for Farrah. His body was like a tuning fork. She was turning out to be what he wanted, and though he knew the consequences of a blooded mate—one who could control him with but a word, the need to put their needs before his own, the willingness to lose his life for hers—he hadn't walked away. He damn sure didn't want to. She was easy to be around and comfortable. Unlike most females, she didn't rub his skin raw with stupid concerns and frivolity. That was probably the worst thing about vamps. Living for so long and being virtually immortal made them the most jaded and cynical creatures. That was something Farrah wasn't.

"So," she said after he was pulling the car onto the chilly Detroit streets from the alley, "what else are we doing?"

"Well, I thought we would start with the club and hang out there for a few hours, then maybe go on a walk near the waterfront to unwind before I get you home at dawn. Sound good?"

"Oh, well... I mean, I guess you could take me home, but I was hoping for something a little more interesting."

"Well, I don't want you to think I'm only into the sex part. I thought we were doing the human thing. You know. Dating."

"Oh, lucky day," she said with a roll of her eyes he imagined based on the sarcasm in her voice. "I would think a male like you rather enjoyed sex twenty-four seven."

Anwar inhaled deeply, the scent of sex seeping into him. She was—or had been—aroused, and it was the best thing he'd scented all night. The thought made him press a little too hard on the gas, sending the squeal of tires out into the night.

"Ah, I hit a nerve, did I?"

"Every now and again, I like to blow the dust off my

engine," he lied. Better that than to admit she had hit one of his buttons.

"You know, you and Leila have this car hobby in common. I never got into it, but I can see the appeal. What made you get into collecting cars?" she asked, not looking at him but out into the brightly lit streets. She had a great memory for recalling that tiny piece of information from his profile. "This one is nice, by the way. What is it?" she asked, looking around at the interior with fascination.

Anwar allowed his fingers to slip over the leather-bound steering wheel. "This is a sixty-six Charger. One of my favorites. It was something to do in a long life of nothing to occupy my time. And there was a market. Much like the VMA, right? You facilitate mating, which is essential for our preservation but quite elusive for our kind, you know? It's an interesting dynamic. So few of us, and so the inability to find your *one* nearly impossible."

"Well, have you *ever* been in love?" she asked, completing the sentence with air quotes.

Anwar saw her expectant look in his periphery and couldn't help but smile. "I have not. It's been a very long time since I thought I could love someone," he said. He ran his fingers through his hair, pushing it back away from his face. Anwar was a goner, and he didn't even mind it. He hadn't expected to like fulfilling his responsibility. But with Farrah, it seemed as if it would be easy.

"Must actually be impossible if a fine, upstanding vampire like yourself has trouble finding a mate." Her voice sounded lower and less confident.

"Maybe not. Maybe I just wasn't looking in the right places," he said.

"Well, that's not my fault," she said. "All the cool kids know about VMA."

A vibrating sound came from her tiny purse. Anwar tried not to watch, forcing his eyes onto the road and away from her extracting her cell phone from her purse. His *kensee* banged around in his chest, aching to claim her. In an instant, he realized he was jealous. Furious over someone intruding on their date. Their time together. He had no right, and until two days ago, he hadn't even wanted a mate. It was a ludicrous notion, and she'd been right. There was no way for him to lay claim to her when he hadn't even figured his own shit out.

When he couldn't take it anymore, he glanced over and found her texting furiously. "Is everything okay?"

"Yeah... I mean, I don't know. I've had... well, you know, some no-shows on dates. The odd thing is, one of them notified us of her location for her meeting. It was with the guy you saw at VMA. Apparently, they were going to meet at Tabernacle tonight. I mean... it's funny that we're going there. Maybe I could ask a bartender or someone if they've seen her?"

Anwar felt like a jackass. There he was being territorial, and she was checking on her clients. "Yeah, if you want, maybe I could introduce you to some of the more popular staff members? They know most of the regulars, and if she frequents Tabernacle, they'll be the ones to tell you."

"I would appreciate that." Farrah slipped her phone back into the compact purse with precision, despite it appearing smaller than the actual cell itself.

"No problem. Whatever you need."

For a while, it was quiet. They continued into the heart of the city to the Tabernacle. The club was below old St. Mary's church downtown. Her eyes widened as they pulled into the parking garage across the street.

"We're going to the casino?" she asked.

"No, it's in the church across the street."

"So, there's a club in a church?"

"Farrah, have you been to any of the vampire clubs? At all?"

"No. We go to human clubs and some of them have vampire rooms if they're owned by one of us."

"Well, this isn't just any old club. You have to be a member. I think you'll enjoy it once you get used to all the sights. Most vampires do, anyway. And there are a few more rules associated with feedings." It was the quintessential sex den, and human pairings were permitted and legal, so long as the humans in attendance were discreet, which meant they would need to leave with virtually no memory of their visit. Only that the *person* who brought them there was a friend. And they had the time of their lives, which would most likely explain the soreness in the most sensitive of places.

Anwar pulled up to a closed-off section of the parking garage. Pressing the call button on the intercom at the gate, he glanced over and gave Farrah a reassuring grin. Her eyes were clouded over with a touch of concern. "You'll be fine, Farrah."

"I hope so, but more and more, I find that I don't fit in the normal spaces. I actually started VMA so I wouldn't have to pretend to be something I'm not," she said in a low voice.

He had to look at her then, because he could not believe what he was hearing. "You must not see the same things I see when you look in the mirror. You don't need to be anything other than what you are. Not for me, anyway." He hadn't known her long enough to drag her into his arms and hold her until she understood how special she was. It hadn't even been long enough for him to want to. But, saints help him, he did. He wanted it all. There was something special about her.

There had been tales of vampire matings that had nothing to do with the blood exchange, but he'd never seen it. Therefore, he hadn't believed it. But now he wasn't so sure.

"If you say so." She smiled a touch. The first one of the evening, and it lit his heart.

"I do."

A static ripple came from the speaker just outside the car. "Tabernacle. State the reason for your visit," asked a French-accented voice.

"It's Archambault Tsedek." That was all he said. It was all he needed to say.

"Archambault?" Farrah asked, the laugh evident in her voice.

Anwar shot her a glance over his shoulder meant to warn her about teasing him for his given name. Her giggle was light and bubbly and gave him yet another warm feeling in the pit of his stomach.

He returned his attention to the speaker system, then looked up at the ball-shaped surveillance device. After a moment of silence, the heavy arm raised into the sky, allowing them entry. Anwar pulled into the darkened section of the garage, down a long row of barricades that made the place look like it was under construction. Past the orange cones, around the other side, there was a dip lower into the earth and a bend around a corner. They turned to find some of the finest automobiles in North America. Some of the heavy hitters must have been out, Anwar thought.

"Tabernacle is probably not what you'd expect,

Farrah. Just thought I'd warn you again before we go in," he said, beginning the trek to the front door and down a set of concrete stairs into what would have been the church cellar ages ago. There would be seven more gates to traverse in the underground tunnels before they arrived. Anwar used the time to explain the rules of the club, such as don't touch anyone unless you want to be touched back, don't drink anything someone proffered without seeing it poured from a bottle behind the bar, don't stray away from the main lighted area without him, and finally, females were often selected for open games. She would need to stick close to Anwar if she didn't want to be selected. Of course, if she did, it was her choice. Something stirred within him at the thought. Well, maybe he would leave that part out.

He was more concerned for his own sake than for hers.

Walking inside, Farrah clung to him a bit. It was a wild scene. They stepped into the room complete with mile-high, arched ceilings and a couple hundred vampires gyrating to grunge music in the smoky den. There were blood fountains on tables scattered through the room. The pungent, coppery scent filled the air as deep red rivulets streamed into waiting champagne glasses. Their source? A human hung from chains, blood flowing into the fountains from the slit wrists.

Anwar looked down at Farrah and found her eyes wide. And staring at the others. There were couples and groups of vampires each doing something that was bound to be illegal in several states under human laws. There was a full-scale orgy in clear view of the main floor being carried out above them. The glass allowed pay-per-view-level voyeurism.

"You okay... or do you want to leave?" This was giving Farrah a front-row seat to the kind of thing Anwar liked. He was into watching. But he would understand if it wasn't her thing.

"Um... well, I think I get why Leila never brought me here. I'm a bit vanilla."

Anwar couldn't help but smile at her. She was almost too good to be true. Anwar had been in few relationships but knew most vampires were cynics. Farrah somehow wasn't. She was refreshing. "That's okay. If you get uncomfortable, let me know and we're out of here."

"Okay." She grabbed his arm tighter and took a step.

"Would you like a drink?" He moved in the direction of the champagne fountain. He picked up a glass and handed it to her.

She took it and drank the entire contents in one swallow. "Thank you." Her voice shook a bit.

"I, uh... I'm not this savage," he told her. "But I do enjoy a bit of sport."

"What, exactly, does that mean?"

For a moment, he hesitated. Being in the room with such carnal desires on display spoke to the beast he'd been trying to control when in her presence. He wanted to curb his base instincts, but they rose and fell inside him with the beat of the music and the pulse of the crowd. "Come with me and I will show you." Extending his hand, he waited to see if she would accept it or run out of the joint screaming.

As her hand met his in unspoken agreement, a knot of tension released, even if he hadn't known it was there. "Okay, I just..." She glanced around the room again. "I just need a minute."

He watched as she lifted her eyes to the throngs of

bodies pressed together overhead. The bewilderment etched in her face clued him in that he'd made an egregious error. The last thing he wanted her to do was enter into something she hadn't been prepared for. He'd just assumed since she ran the VMA, she would have been versed in the varied ways vampires amused themselves. She had been at Frank's place. Just the look on her face told him he'd made the wrong assumption. "We don't have to do this. If you would prefer—"

"Are you a Dom? Or a voyeur?"

It stung for a moment. His hunch from moments ago was validated. It was new for vampires to have any sense of pious behavior. Most vampires gave themselves over to their desires since most of their fear died the night of their transition. "I am so many things, Farrah. Let's get you some air, shall we?"

She hadn't released his hand, so he guided her back through the maze of people. Once on the other side of the hidden passageway into the club, he stopped. He wanted her to make the decision on the next step. He would love to stay, to be with her in a space where he could be himself with this female who was so very intriguing. But it would have to be her choice. He hadn't expected her reaction, but he did respect it.

"So, what does 'a lot of things' mean?"

"Just that I'm someone who enjoys the act of submission. I enjoy watching others have sex. And I especially enjoy a bit of rough play. One of the best things about being an immortal is our propensity for pain and pleasure. I—I wanted to offer you a glimpse of my life."

"And telling me exactly what this place was hadn't blipped on your radar? Not that I'm a prude, I just need to be sure about what I'm doing."

The center of his chest tightened a bit as she walked away from him. He thought for a moment about what he wanted—rather needed—to say to her to help her see he wasn't trying to ambush her. What he actually wanted was to expose his soul to her. If she was the type of female who could deal with some of his darker desires, then perhaps she would be the type to understand who and what he was. "I didn't mean to startle you. I don't think you're uptight. I just maybe misunderstood just how much you've experienced in your lifetime."

"Oh, don't get me wrong. I've seen a lot, but humans hanging from their ankles in the middle of a sex den is a lot." She shook her head and ran a hand over the back of her neck.

"The humans you saw, they are not willing. But they are those who would do harm. Humans who have done terrible things and... alas, won't be missed. It's more of a public service."

"Oh well, I guess the vigilante memo was missed."

"Leila hasn't told you about this?"

She looked at him and shifted away, her body language indicating discomfort? Perhaps confusion. "She has not."

"Well..." Anwar stopped. The last thing he wanted to do was drive a wedge between Farrah and her maker. "I'm sure she has her reasons."

"I guess..." She held her head down for a moment, probably running her mind over the thoughts that would lead her to Lelia's reasons for keeping certain things from her. Grabbing at her skirt that looked to be from medieval times but was still sexy as hell, she patted herself, up the stunningly adorned bustier. "Fuck. I left my purse in your car."

"C'mon, we can go back if you want."

"No, it's fine. You stay and I'll go back to grab it. I'll be right back, and we can, um... give your little voyeur thing a try." She bit her lower lip and glanced up from lowered lids.

In an instant, his cock was engaged. His body reacted to her like a beacon. "No, I'm walking you back. I wouldn't trust these bastards around someone as gorgeous as you are." He'd been good most of the night, so he took the opportunity to pull her close, like something precious he needed to keep on his person. The long walk with her tucked under his arm and his palm pressed near the small of her back seemed too short as they neared his car.

He slipped a hand in his pocket and retrieved the key fob he'd had the car retrofitted with as he followed behind her. The chirp sang out into the night air.

Slowly, Farrah turned and walked away, tossing a seductive glance over her shoulder. Anwar watched, captivated as she moved her gloriously curvy body across the parking lot. She flipped her hair, the curls landing over her shoulder as she reached to open the car door.

Despite him not having touched the alarm again, he heard a sound, like a whirring noise. Then it came again, probably milliseconds after the first sound, but with his heightened sense of hearing, he had time to listen and assign a source. In his dealings with the Order, there were many who had been eliminated on their demands. He'd seen many explosive devices in the surveillance films time and time again. He'd seen how they worked. Knew what the right kinds of production materials could do to all sorts of immortals. And could pick the sound of one about to go off in a wind tunnel, let alone in an empty parking lot with someone who was starting to mean so much to him. There was something attached to his car, and it was about to go off.

"Wait," Anwar screamed, charging across the cracked concrete. The only thing he could think of was getting her to safety. The ominous click sounded out again, and in less time than it took to blink, Farrah could be gone.

As he reached her, the heat from the blast licked at his flesh before the sound did. Debris flew at him from everywhere as he cradled her in his arms, tucked her close to his chest, and flew as far as he could away from the blast. It was haphazard and messy. Crossing the short distance was not handled with any of his normal grace. His mind tripped over who would do such a thing. And as he crashed to the ground with Farrah beneath him, he looked down at her. Her face and neck were bloody, her skin burned off in places. She moaned in his arms, half unconscious and dazed from the blast. He hadn't made it to her in time, and it was something he would never forgive himself for.

He also knew in that desperate moment, he would destroy whoever was responsible.

CHAPTER SIXTEEN

Farrah blinked, then again to find herself in a foreign bed. Her first instinct was to sit up. As she did, pain exploded from every part of her body, and she immediately collapsed back into the pillows, slamming her eyes shut.

"Don't try to move," a deep, raspy voice said.

"Yup, got that." She squinted to see who was talking to her and found Anwar sitting on the edge of the bed. "Where are we?"

"My penthouse. I brought you back here after... everything went down."

Everything went down? Searching her mind, she started to remember. There had been a bright light just before everything went o'dark thirty. "What's everything? And take it slow. I'm a bit blurry." The worst pain was in her head. Reaching a hand up, she touched the sore spot and found a large knot on her forehead. Wincing, she realized moving and touching things probably wasn't the best idea.

"I was watching you walk to my car, and it exploded after I hit the alarm. Thankfully, I heard the mechanism trigger and got to you before... well, before it killed you. From what I could tell, it wasn't very professional. My car took the worst of it."

"Your car is so beautiful, though." Farrah wasn't quite ready for prime time. It even hurt to think. "Why aren't you hurt?"

Her question was met with silence that lasted so long, she attempted to open her eyes again, if only to check whether he was still there.

"Because... I'm not like you, Farrah."

Anwar's bedroom wasn't what she'd imagined. He should have been laid up in something similar to a panty-snatching lair. Deuce Bigalow sprang to mind, and wasn't the main gigolo named Anwar, too?

She returned her attention to him and found him patiently waiting for her to respond. Her head swam, and she needed to focus on something other than her interest in him, no matter how fish-grease hot he was. "Anwar, I don't know how long I'm going to be conscious, and I want to tell you something before I pass out again. I think someone is targeting vampire females. Myself included."

Anwar's eyes widened, lips pressed paper-thin despite their fullness. Rubbing a hand on the back of his neck, he looked off as if he wanted to be anywhere else at the moment. "What? I mean, a car blew up, but I thought it was about me—"

"I mean, think about it. I got a text on the way there that one of my clients had been at the same club. She misses her date and then your car is blown to smithereens? It feels like too much of a coincidence."

Anwar stared off for a moment, obviously putting some things together. "Who would want to harm you? Do you have any enemies? As hard as that is to imagine, I have to ask."

"No... I mean, VMA is illegal in the eyes of the Order. But they don't know we exist, or if they do, they haven't seemed to care."

"We don't have to talk about all that right now, Farrah," he said.

"Oh, I'm sorry. I cut you off. What did you have to tell me?"

Anwar paused again, as if he had been taken off guard. "You know, it can wait. Let's just make sure you're doing better. Then we can talk."

Farrah started to prod him. Anwar didn't seem to be one who opened up easily, but she could wait. In fact, she worried that she could wait forever for him. And wondered whether he felt the same way.

A rap on the door barged into her thoughts. "Hello, kids. I can't say for sure, but I'm guessing you all aren't the king and queen of the homecoming dance. I've heard of being unpopular, but this is ridiculous."

Farrah brought her head around to find Mael, but a sharp pain had her laid out on the bed again. "I don't think this is the time for jokes." She still didn't quite trust him since Leila hated him, but Anwar seemed to rely on him completely.

His presence brought her attention to something else. For the first time, she thought of what she might be wearing. Glancing down, she found a shirt several times too large. It was one of Anwar's, a gray button-down that smelled of his heavenly scent. While she wasn't wearing anything else, the heavy duvet covered everything below her waist, thankfully.

"Oh, come, come now. We have to laugh to keep from crying. I am truly glad no harm came to you, however."

"Me too," she said, trying once again to sit upright and remain that way.

"I need to call a meeting of the Order." Anwar's voice boomed in the room, the sound bouncing from wall to wall.

Did he just say... No matter how bad the pain, a full-on brilliant explosion of needle pricks and burning on her back, Farrah sat upright on the bed. "Is this about what you wanted to tell me before?"

"I was trying to tell you—"

Mael cleared his throat. "Not sure what he was going to tell you, but his father is a council member. Anwar is his proxy during his long-term absence. When he returns, Constantine will resume his role. In the interim, think of Anwar as a stand-in."

"What the fuck are you saying?" Her heart drummed in her chest, and she followed her first instinct to get off the bed and get the hell out. She tried to stand, but her legs gave way. Anwar caught her before she could even hit the bed. "Anwar, let go of me," she demanded, struggling free of his grasp even if almost every bone in her body hurt.

He moved away and held his hands up in surrender as he took two steps back. "Farrah... Technically, I'm not a member of the Order. I'm covering for my father."

"So, it's possible that they tried to kill me for having VMA?"

"No, of course not. They haven't enforced those rules in ages," Anwar said.

Glancing between Mael and Anwar, she tried to read their body language. Mael appeared pensive, and Anwar just looked lost.

"From what I hear, the Order is filled with monsters. So they could have," she said.

"Again," Anwar started, but not before kneeling on the floor before her. "In all fairness, I'm rather different from the other members. More progressive and less structured, or so I've been told. To be frank, I despise talking to them any more than I have to. For the first time, however, I can see their usefulness."

"But you lied to me. How can I know..." A sharp pain stabbed at her chest, and she wasn't sure what caused it— an injury from the explosion or Anwar singlehandedly blowing up her life. She rubbed at the ache and shook her head. "I don't even know where I stand. If this is going to ruin me."

"I know you're angry with me," Anwar said, desperation hitched in his voice. "But I will make sure that no one harms you. Not ever again." He shifted his position to face Mael. "Get them on the phone and tell them we need a meeting. Tonight."

"Are you sure you want to involve them?" Mael flexed his jaw and crossed his arms in front of himself, one of the first times Farrah had seen him take on a more serious tone.

While she had never met any of the Order's members before, based on what Leila had said, they weren't the good-time gang. She pulled in a deep inhale that reminded her she wasn't healed just yet. Her idea to get up had been the wrong one, and she leaned back onto the pillows at gingerly as possible.

Anwar moved forward on his knees, somehow still

over her as he positioned the pillows behind her head. When he was done, he grabbed her hand. "I promise, I wasn't expecting to like anyone at VMA. Lying to you wasn't my end game. It's just that when females find out who my family is and the seat my father holds, they tend to come up with assumptions about who I am. I would rather someone get to know me for me."

As much as Farrah hated to admit it, she knew how hard it was to make an impression on someone. It was one of the founding principles of VMA. They weren't done talking about his omission, but there were more pressing matters at play. "Okay, but we are going to discuss this, Anwar. It's not cool," she said, motioning between the two of them and feeling wholly like a fool.

"I never told them about VMA. And I won't. This was not some ploy to harm you. I hope you'll give me a chance to show you." In that moment, he looked so earnest, so concerned. But hadn't he before?

Unable to look into his eyes anymore, Farrah pulled her hand away from Anwar and turned to Mael. "If dealing with them is troublesome, there may be other ways to track down who did this."

Mael only shook his head and nodded to Anwar, redirecting her attention back to the last male she wanted to focus on. He was so beautiful. And at the moment, he represented yet another mistake.

Grave eyes raked over her face as he covered her hand with his. "Trust me, I would not be doing this if they weren't so resourceful. There are politicians, executives, even stars on the take from Order members. While I'm sure we could slug away collecting information, they will get it for us easier. The explosion could serve as a threat to humans discovering who we are. That will motivate them to help, more than anything."

"I'll call it in. Once I do, though, we'll need to go to the chambers immediately," Mael said.

"Do you think Leila can come stay with you?" Anwar's expression hadn't lightened yet.

"I'll call her." Farrah had to fight the urge to give in to sleep as it pulled at her. She hadn't expected the gut-punch from Anwar, and with the injuries, she was barely hanging on.

"No, I'll call her if you give me her number. I'll leave word with the doorman if she gets here after we're gone already. He has an extra key."

He must have been well and truly wealthy. There was rich, then there was this. Rich was the least of his problems. He was also a liar. More than anything, she was concerned with what they would do to her about VMA. What it could mean for Leila and her businesses. And alas, despite his lies, she didn't want anything to happen to Anwar, either. She had heard so many vile things... that they were treacherous people with no souls, heartless and vindictive. "Are you sure this is the only thing that can be done?"

"I know you don't know me well, but this is the best possible way. I will make sure no harm comes to you. This I swear to you, Farrah. I don't believe they did this, and I need access to their information to find out who did. They have the entire city's resources at their disposal. Maybe they can finally put it to good use."

"All right, but I can't just sit here doing nothing. I'm going to ping my tech guy and find out if he has more leads. There must be a way they are getting into my system to find their targets. To find me."

There was a sick feeling in the pit of her belly. Perhaps it was just a result of the searing pain shooting up and down her legs and back. Or maybe it was the freshly ripped hole in her heart. It would be a while before her vampire healing kicked in. And she would need to feed in order to accelerate it. Yet again, she was relying on Anwar when she didn't even know who he was.

"You need to feed."

"And I will. It's just that I think you do too. There are consequences to that."

"Ahem, you want me to wait outside for this," Mael cut in.

Dammit, she'd forgotten he was even in the room. "No—"

"Yes," Anwar cut in.

"Oookkkkay. I'll be downstairs, Anwar. I will alert the Order." With that, Mael turned on his heel and left the room.

She hadn't wanted to be an inconvenience in Anwar's life. She wasn't the type of female to come between friends. "It's okay, you can just go."

"No," he growled, his eyes glowing in silvery blue. "I do not need to feed. You, however, need to heal. I would have given you my blood had you been conscious enough to drink."

"Without my consent?"

"Absolutely. I would save your life without permission. You've been out since the explosion. A full twenty-four hours. Your injuries are not healing on their own. This is not a debate."

She released a sigh. This was the worst possible situation. Part of her was already forgiving him. Some blind hope that he was actually the man he purported himself to be. "I don't want to do this, but I need to know if any of my clients are wrapped up in this mess. If I do, please don't think this means we are back to the dating thing. It will take me a while to get past this, if I even can."

"Understood. But you will drink today." The timbre of his voice was at a previously unknown level of deep. He sounded predatory and virile. Using one of his pre-extended fangs, he slit his wrist and held it out for her.

The unfortunate thing was, despite her proclivity to argue with him on things she didn't want to do, hunger swelled inside her at the sight of the sustenance. Normally, she would have said no, but the natural instincts for a vampire to feed took over. The shift from civil to ferocious struck, compelling her to take from him, the hunger so intense, none of the pain or discomfort registered in her brain. With one fluid movement, she latched to his vein.

As her mouth closed over his wrist, his heady juices tasting of the most exotic spices, her body thrummed with energy. With power. She pulled deeper, and all control slipped away from her the more she drank. Farrah had never been so needy to have a male inside her. This new place was uncharted territory. She was all-in.

With both hands, she pulled his arm closer to her mouth, lost in the eroticism of the act. She was more than feeding. Farrah was on the verge of ingesting his soul, if such a thing could happen. She'd forgotten about the anger, if only for a moment, to be lost in the churning tide of lust.

"Easy now, Farrah. My blood is potent and should be taken in measure." Though Anwar's voice was right near her ear, she heard it from far away.

The feral being she'd become in the moment grabbed

at his cock, taking its girth in her hands. The mass of it pulsed against her palm through his pants. The only thing keeping her from climbing on top of him and taking her fill was the need for his blood.

A groan came from his chest as a hand grappled onto her neck and brought her head up to meet his fiery, desperate eyes. "You aren't fully healed, Farrah."

She could sense his strain in efforts to resist her, but she would not have it. She wanted him with everything inside her, just as he desired her. "I'm not going to take no for an answer, Anwar. I could have been killed, so I'm not in the mood to take moments for granted." On a fresh surge of lust and desire, she pushed forward, freeing herself from his grip, and pressed him back onto the bed. With new energy, she pinned his hands over his head. Grinding her heated core against him only made her need worse.

"I cannot resist if you keep this up, and I don't want to take advantage of this situation," he said.

Lifting slightly, she inquired about the only thing that would or could make her stop. "I'm on fire for you. You don't want me? Don't want this?" Her voice was a feline purr, and she climbed his body, straddling him before leaning forward then pressing her hungry mouth against his.

"I—goddammit, I don't want you to regret this moment when the effects of the feeding wear off. And I also don't want to hurt you."

"Nor I you. Let us have this. If we are fighting for our lives in whatever this is, it may be our last time." As morbid as the revelation was, it only served to thrust them together. She did not even have the presence of mind to remind him not to bite her, for they could not spare an ounce of the strength that would be sapped in their mating. Even if her skin felt on the verge of combustion for his fangs to be buried deep in her flesh.

Hooded eyes stared back at her. It was as if she could see any fight or resistance seep away into the abyss of their yearning. A corded arm went around her back before flipping her.

He rose and stripped away his T-shirt and pants, leaving behind a mountain of masculinity that made her mouth go dry. She longed for him, her body crying to be pleasured with all he had to give again and again.

At once, he was on top of her, his finger finding her sensitive clit before slipping inside her wetness. "This will be mine," he said, his voice reverberating in his body like a tuning fork.

"And this..." She reached down between them and grabbed the cock too big to hold in one hand, grappled it, and squeezed. "This is mine whenever I want it."

A roar tore from him as he extracted the fingers occupying the space and replaced it with every inch of his manhood.

She cried out his name, clutching at him. Her attempts were met with a strong hand that wrapped around her wrist and pinned her, the other grasping a thigh and lifting it to his shoulder. He spanked her ass with a sinister smile and went down to latch on to her breast, lapping at it like a starved man.

The movement allowed him to fill her completely, to reach depths no male had ever. Warm tears slid over her cheeks as she rode him, her pleasure taking control.

Their world was uncertain, and the next moments were not promised until they figured out what was happening around them. None of that mattered at the moment, though. Nothing was as urgent, as important, as their bodies being joined together in utter bliss. She needed him, right where he was.

Everything else, whatever it was, whatever they did to one another, would have to wait.

CHAPTER SEVENTEEN



*T*he trek across town to that fucker Anwar's place took too damned long. He had already waited a whole night to reach out to her. She had assumed Farrah and Anwar had spent the day together but not because she'd been hurt.

Leila had been checking her bars all the way on the deep Northwest side. It was a Friday night, too risky for her to attempt flying since people routinely used drones downtown near Anwar's place to record baseball games, fireworks, and whatever the hell else got humans off. With no other options, she was left with driving there. *Fuck.* She mentally cursed and banged the steering wheel with every stop-and-go movement from traffic on the 96 free-way. Fucking Michigan and its perpetual construction season. Despite not having any fucks left, they were sure flying out of her mouth with regularity. She wasn't herself when it came to her friends. Let alone a member of her family, like Farrah.

When she made it to I94 and found yet another pile-up of traffic, she gave up. With an aggressive maneuver, she cut off a semi-truck and pulled up on the exit closest to the casinos. She pulled into the sky-high parking deck and once at the top, she left her car. The winds were high up there, which would only help her move faster. In the blink of an eye, she flew into the sky, careful to hit the sweet spot between airplanes and the normal elevation for drones.

It worked, but thanks to the traffic, it had still taken her an hour to get there, despite it being the middle of the night. Humans and their goddamn sports and festivals. But she had remembered the blood bags from the cellar of her club. They weren't optimal, but they were useful.

She tore into the parking garage of Anwar's downtown residence nearly breaking the heels of her favorite shoes. Half in a parking space and sideways, she slammed the bags into her purse and practically levitated inside and through the entryway, only stopping because she needed the security guard to give her the key. He was a gangly human with fire-red hair and freckles dusted over his face. "Anwar Tsedek left me a key here. I'm Le—"

Green eyes flicked somewhere past her. Before she could turn around, she heard the voice that made her flesh crawl. And her core perk up.

"It's okay, Sebastian. I'll take her up."

She would flay Anwar, not only for allowing Farrah to get hurt, but also for allowing her to walk into a meeting with that bastard, Maelstrom. On a turn, she took a deep breath and squinted at him. "Well, what's taking you so long?"

He didn't argue with her, though the set of his jaw lent to him holding back a mouthful. "Right this way, Leila. She's waiting for you." He took a deep inhale when she drew closer to him, then when she walked right past him toward the elevator, he used the one angel strength she hated. Telepathically, his words whispered across her mind. "You should not walk around with bags of blood. If anyone had caught you for—"

She shut down her brain, effectively blocking him out. Normally, it would have taken concentration, but as mad as she was, all it took was merely a thought of the action. "Don't do that again," she barked, pressing the up button the moment she got there.

"I was only trying to help, dear one," he said. He was right behind her and she could smell the ocean scent of him, feel the angelic magic washing over her with the same intensity as the day he'd walked out on her.

"Give me the apartment and leave me, *fallen*." Sure, it was a low blow, and he had ended up losing his home, the sanctity of Heaven he purported it to be in punishment for whatever he'd done for his brother. The bastard would have never fallen for her. Hearing about his fall from one of her friends on the DL probably hurt worse than anything else. Even more than the day he'd left her.

"I have the key. And something tells me they won't be in any position to open the door for you." As if on cue, the elevator doors opened. His hand pressed into her low back and sent shivers over her.

Snatching away, she practically threw herself into the corner, as far away from him as she could get. The scents of sex and lust wafted through the air. Not only was her bestie, the one she would have ripped an arm off for, up in a penthouse screwing instead of recovering, but Mael had the audacity to put a hand on her.

"If you touch me again, I'm going to kill you, Mael. I'm not even joking a little bit," she said through gritted teeth.

He didn't turn around to face her. Instead, he inserted a key and turned before pressing the highest number on the keypad. The cart began moving before he spoke again. "I know you will, Leila. Can't blame a guy for trying."

She refused to respond. There was not a single breath she wanted to waste on him. She'd done enough of that after everything had gone down. Enough talking. Too many tears had been shed. She had sworn no one would ever get close enough to make her feel that way again. Without the pain he'd inflicted, she would have never turned anyone. And while her actions had left her vulnerable, her children had given her a reason to live. Now, VMA clients were coming up missing and Farrah had nearly been killed. All of it seemed to correlate with his arrival. It was too much of a coincidence. And if she found out he had something to do with it, she would do him as she'd promised. She cursed under her breath at the thought.

Thankfully for him, the elevator opened to the most opulent living room she'd seen in at least a century. Ornate art and antique furnishings filled out the spacious room. It was a completely open space, the kitchen and dining area overlooking the entire city. She had never been inside the Westborn but had heard it was owned by a vampire with ridiculous wealth and a penchant for isolation. All of it smelled of heartbreak for Farrah.

"Where is she?"

Mael walked around her over to a couch laden with

gold adornments. "She's in there. I'd knock first."

Leila didn't need to. She could scent the sex, along with Farrah, in the air. If she would have used her maker's bond, she probably would have known her exact position in the place. Who needed that shit, though? It was already upsetting. No need to add more fuel to the fire.

She didn't have to wait long. Anwar emerged from a door on the opposite side of the room. With no time wasted, Leila strode over to him and met him eye to eye. Well, almost. The fucker was freakishly tall. Like some kind of giant. "If my progeny has one hair out of place, I will snatch your arms from your body and beat you to death with them."

Anwar stepped back, nearly dragging her with him. She hadn't even realized she was standing on his toes until he moved away. "She is fine. I fed her. All her wounds are healing."

"You fed her?" Seeing red, she lashed out, fangs extended, and swiped at him with claw-like nails.

Not fast enough, though, because in one movement, he was behind her, arms caging her against the wall. "We are not blood-mated, Leila. I haven't taken her blood."

"You had better not," she bit out, struggling against the monster to get free.

"I'm going to let you go, but you have to promise not to attack me... or Mael, for that matter."

"Fine." She jostled again. Using all her strength, she pushed against immovable arms. "Fine, I said."

"Okay, I'm trusting you." Slowly, he lowered his arms. "We only helped her. She's not hurt badly. I—"

Leila turned around to face him, only barely able to focus from her anger. "You what?"

"I shielded her with my body from the explosion. I

heard the ignition moments before it went off. Most of her injuries were from the impact and me falling on top of her."

"Then why aren't you hurt?" she asked, looking him up and down. Despite being immortal, vampires were not impervious to being wounded. It just took a lot more for them to die.

"I'm old. I heal faster." He turned away from her and walked to the couch opposite Mael. The pair looked at one another as if communicating, though neither of their mouths moved.

Knowing of Mael's powers, she stalked toward them. "What aren't you telling me?" She looked to Anwar, still not ready to deal with Mael.

"Farrah believes the females who missed their dates are actually... well, missing. There could be other races involved too, but we don't know for sure. We're going to the Order to get some help."

"They're waiting for us, by the way," Mael chimed in.

"Those assholes won't help anyone but themselves." That part, she knew with certainty.

"We need access to traffic cams, intel on any known militias or cells moving against immortals. We won't be able to find as many resources in one place. Trust me, I hate them too. But what other choice do we have? And I need you to stay with Farrah until we return." Anwar looked up at her with his brow furrowed, and that's when she knew.

Most immortals were afraid if they had to go before the Order. Anwar was just pissed. She didn't sense caution nor concern rolling off him. Only anger. There it was. Two and two came together in her mind to equal all kinds of bullshit. "You muthafucker. I knew I didn't like you. And what should I have expected since you hang out with this POS?" She waved a hand in Mael's direction.

"Careful, darling. It's a thin line between love and hate. You'll end up in my bed if you aren't wary," Mael said.

In unison, both Anwar and Leila shouted, "Shut up, Mael."

"Now isn't the time, brother," Anwar said.

"You're a member of the Order, aren't you?" She could have spit and the words wouldn't have come out harsher.

"I am a proxy for my father."

She leveled a glare at Mael.

"Don't look at me. I'm not a card carrier. They have yet to invite me to the barbeque."

"Does Farrah know? Because I can't imagine she would have screwed you if she had."

"Maybe not the first time," Mael said. "But I think this last time, she was fully aware. Isn't that right, Anwar?"

"You are not helping," Anwar bit out.

Anger ripped through Leila anew, and she turned away from the less-than-dynamic duo and marched in the direction of the room Anwar had come out of.

Barging in, she slammed the door behind her and found a freshly sated Farrah sprawled across a luxurious bed, tangled in messy, fucked-on sheets. "Have you lost your mind?"

Behind her, she heard the ding of the elevator. In front of her, the person Leila would have bled out for voluntarily stared at her with the look of sorry-not-sorry written all over her face.

*Well, ain't that a bitch.*

## CHAPTER EIGHTEEN

Reluctantly, Anwar loaned Farrah his computer so she could check on VMA and her clients. After adjusting the brightness on the Mac, she could finally look at it. The first message in her portal was from Ennis, asking her to call him when she could.

Within a few seconds of messaging him, she received a Zoom link, which he answered with bed-head hair and the same disheveled hot-boy look he always sported.

"Wow, girl. Looking awesome," he cracked.

"I could say the same for you, my friend." She chuckled, but immediately regretted it due to the pounding in her brain.

"Touché. Well, it took me a few days, but I've pinpointed the location of the guy who hacked your servers. It wasn't even a hack. He created a fake profile and set up dates the first time. Then there's someone named isabelle549, whose profile has been accessed from the same IP. Looks like humans are responsible, and based on the shitty firewalls, they aren't professionals, just lucky. I'm uploading this info to your email now. And that

Eire chick... The GPS to the location was provided on her calendar in the app like I told you, but it looks like she never showed. Not sure if you knew, so just wanted to give you the most up-to-date info I could," Ennis said.

"And she hasn't checked in again? Look for time and date stamps in the back of her profile."

"I did," he said. Farrah could hear light clicks from his side of the connection. "Just checked again, and nothing."

Before Farrah could ask any more questions, the door of Anwar's bedroom blew open, banging against the wall. For a moment, Farrah was afraid whoever had blown up Anwar's car had found them. In the aftermath, there was just a very pissed-off-looking Leila. *Shit...*

"I'll call you back." Farrah ended the call with Ennis and placed the laptop beside her in the mess of blankets.

"What the hell are you doing, Farrah?"

Farrah pulled the covers up over her chest. Since Leila was her maker, Farrah felt the inherent need to make her happy. As a child would her mother. She shook her head to clear those thoughts since she'd done nothing wrong. "What do you mean?"

Leila sniffed at the air. "It smells like Moulin Rouge up in here. Not even a full day after you almost died in the most violent of ways, you're in here beneath a member of the Order? You do realize they could have been the ones targeting you in one of their fucked-up vendettas, don't you?"

While Farrah felt amazing, she honestly didn't have the strength to fight with Leila. Not when Anwar turned out to be everything she'd warned Farrah about. "I know. We aren't mated, though." Although a stirring in her gut began the moment she mentioned him. Anwar was probably going to turn out to be a huge regret of hers.

"Yeah, well, that is just one of the universe's mercies. They aren't the type of males we need in our lives, trust me."

Just by looking at Leila, Farrah knew she wasn't going to hear her out. She was positively glowering, arms crossed tightly over her chest. "Okay, you can mom the shit out of me later. I found something out. Give me a second to get dressed, and I'll come out and we can talk about it, okay?"

"Fine." Leila rolled her eyes. Digging deep into a leather messenger bag she had strapped across her body, she pulled out a blood bag and clothing. "I figured since you'd been in an explosion while hanging out with Anwar, you'd need clothes and feeding. But, from the scent of this place, I'd say those needs are met. I'll be outside on one of those ridiculous couches." She tossed the outfit on the bed with more force than needed, then blew out of the door in the same tornado-like fashion she'd entered with.

"Hmmmmppphhh," Farrah groaned, rolling over and tossing the blood bag, then grabbing the shirt from the top of the pile. She pulled it on after removing Anwar's shirt. She could still smell his masculine scent as she jostled the cover and got dressed.

She needed to stand to put on the jeans. That was when she realized she probably wasn't fully healed. Her knees buckled, forcing her to grab onto the bedpost to stabilize herself. The room rotated around her for a moment, and she shuttered her eyes until her head didn't feel like she was in a Tilt-a-Whirl. She had to seek purchase on the bed as a wave of nausea hit. In a moment, the feeling subsided, and if she had time, she probably would have lain back down. Anwar's blood was potent and amazing, but it wouldn't put the humpty back in her dumpty, especially after the mind-blowing sex session they'd had. His dick was magical, but she could still feel the aftereffects of their lovemaking in addition to the sting of healing on her back and thighs.

But there wasn't time to sit back and nurse her wounds. Anwar had asked her to stay put until he had more info, but it wasn't going to happen. She needed to find out what was happening to her clients, and now Eire might be missing, as well. Gathering herself, she finished dressing and found the stiletto heels from the night before. There was no way her hamstrings were ready for those numbers, so she strung the straps between her fingers and headed out of the room.

Holy crap, she had seen the bedroom, so undoubtedly the rest of the house was immaculate, but she hadn't expected it to be so stately. On the walls were paintings that should have been in museums. Clearly, Anwar had a thing for the early impressionists because there was one from Bazille and another from Gleyre. Sisley and Renoir. When one lived as long as vampires, they could have easily been friends of his. Especially since she'd never seen some of these paintings. For all she knew, they may have given them to him as gifts. Shit, he seemed rich enough to run in all kinds of circles over the course of his lifetime.

The furniture put her store to shame. Everything was from the eighteen hundreds and in perfect condition. Who was Anwar Tsedek? One day, she would have to sit down and talk to him about all that. But not today.

"Okay, Leila," she said, closing the door and leaving the scene of her crime behind her.

Leila was by the floor-to-ceiling windows, staring out

at a sea of city lights. Anwar's view overlooked the Detroit River and the Ambassador Bridge. The city was breathtaking from that level. "So, shall we plan the bridal shower? Since you're acting like a teenaged human."

"Girl, I am sorry. I didn't expect to—"

"To slip up and fall on his dick?"

It was like a slap in the face, and Farrah took a step back, having never been the beneficiary of Leila's sharp tongue. "You mad at me about this? For real?"

"I'm more disappointed," she said, dejection heavy in her voice. "You knew he was a danger, but you still let him spill his seed in you."

"I swear to God, I hate it when you use that judgy-ass Victorian tone."

"It's Regency. You were never any good at history."

"Are you mad at me, or is this about Mael? Because I'm pretty sure you've slept with worse than a member of the Order."

"Oh, that's where we are?" Leila turned around to face her for the first time since Farrah had stepped from the bedroom.

"I guess or whatever. No cap. You are coming at me like you didn't know I was looking for someone to love me."

"You had that already. I think you're just looking for dick, Farrah. I swear, you get like this every time. Remember Ibiza? I practically have to pry you away from that male." Her eyes had fire in them, and in yet another first for the night, there was no evidence of kindness in them.

"You want to talk about what Ennis found out, or continue down this path that might end up somewhere we don't want to be?" As hurtful as Leila's words had been, Farrah was not about to lose sight of her goal. There could be a mountain of dead vampires, and for all she knew, she was next on the list. Some things were more important than Leila's distrust of males. It was about time she knew that.

"Yup. That's cool. But when this is over, I am done with this, Farrah."

Perhaps that was the deadliest jab. Farrah couldn't believe they were falling out over a male, but then again, she'd been batting zero with relationships for her entire existence. Just because Leila had turned her didn't mean she was a true friend, no matter how long they'd known one another. Maybe it was time Farrah realized that. "Okay. He is texting you the location of the IP that hacked VMA. Apparently, there is a link to their server, whoever they are. It's owned by a human male by the name of Billy McDermott."

"Why is he texting me?"

"Because my phone has been blown to smithereens. It's the same reason I didn't call you when I came to. But, you didn't ask about that did you? Healing fine by the way. Thanks for asking."

"Figured, since you'd just finished rolling around that big-ass bed with your knees pinned to your ears. C'mon. I'm driving. And where the fuck are your shoes?"

Farrah looked down at her bare feet sinking into overly plush white carpet. "We need to stop by my place and get some. I can't walk in these right now," she said, holding out the glittering shoes.

Leila rolled her eyes again before fishing the phone from the purse. She pulled it out and made a few swipes at the screen. "This is in the old Packard Plant. That thing is crumbling to the ground. Is Ennis sure?"

"Well, if you're going to maim and torture, what better place than one where nobody would look?"

"I guess you're right." Leila allowed her eyes to roam around Anwar's place for a second. "Think he has any weapons in here?"

"How the hell would I know? Look, we're just going to poke around a little. Probably won't even lead to anything."

"Right... you've been spot-on in the past, so no need to take precautions, huh? We'll stop by Melody. Mike the Bartender has a bag of tricks in his locker that he thinks I don't know about. And you can get yourself a pair of shoes. Let's go," Leila said, then marched right past Farrah.

Something told Farrah it was going to be a long-ass night.

## CHAPTER NINETEEN

He hadn't been in the audience hall of the Order of Immortals in over a year, despite Constantine having gone to rest. It had been by design and most of the time, he'd just called in via conference call. Something this important, though, needed to be requested in person. The hall consisted of regular citizens of each race who had asked to meet with seated Order members. It wasn't his favorite place, but none of that mattered. He had driven an hour to avoid being sighted by drones. They were becoming more and more of a nuisance, thanks to the humans and their damned automation.

The castle was disguised as a mansion, high gates and morbid gray, stone walls to prevent the unlikely assault of hunters or humans. Humans thought most supernatural rumors were no more than fantasized lore. Hunters were bred, and as popular fiction and culture evolved, fewer and fewer believed at all.

While the threat to the paranormals' existence had

been mostly neutralized just under a hundred years ago, the stronghold remained on the outskirts of Port Huron, a Michigan town mostly known for its alternative access to the Canadian border. Despite being mostly used for meetings, the whole place still stank of copper and malice. Granted, it was an old building, but some of its stench was due to the many members of the supernatural races who had been tortured, their blood left behind to soak into the walls. Atlanteans had not been part of the massacres, however. They mostly voted against and were always outnumbered. There was nothing to be gained by killing one another.

Taking a deep breath in through the nose, out through the mouth to keep his usual disdain for every single member in check, Anwar walked into the bowels of the building, where the committee chambers were. He stepped inside through wide-open wooden doors and found six of the members present, only half of them represented.

Viktoria, the elected head of the Order, was there, done up like a Disney villain in an ermine stole and a sparkling black evening gown. Her neck and ears were adorned with diamonds, probably stolen with her own hands from some dynasty or another.

Next to her was Engar, leader of the werewolf clans. He was probably the least happy to be there. He'd never been a fan of Anwar.

Tarik, the exalted ruler of the high fae, had a team of sprints fluttering around his seat. If there were any of them who leaned closest to Atlanteans, it would be the fae. They were big on staying out of shit belonging to others.

The rest were Esmerella of the sirens, Zaria, ordained minister of the shifters—not to be confused with the werewolves because they hated that shit—and finally, Haster, the leader of the demons. He was the mortal enemy of Mael. Rumors had floated around for years about his role in Mael's falling. Either way, Mael had never forgiven the devil his sins.

Anwar stepped onto the table arching outward from the center of the room. Standing on the pentagram in the middle, a place that neutralized the powers upon entry, he waited for acknowledgment. He was not acting as a member at the moment since he entreated assistance. It was part of the many millions of fucking rules. Any immortal seeking help would ask like any other being, so as to prevent corruption amongst the members. It had worked... for the most part. At least according to Constantine.

"The emergency meeting of the Order is now in session. This male, Anwar Tsedek, requests access to the records and assets belonging to this body for immediate and personal use. The purpose of this meeting, at quorum excluding the Tsedek faction, is to decide whether to allocate precious resources for his use or to deny his appeal." Esmerella spoke in formal terms. The role of secretary suited her, if for no other reason than her lack of knowledge around dialect. Sirens were not known for their small talk.

"All right, Anwar. You may state your case before this governing body. And thanks so much for pulling me away from Diddy's rooftop party. I would have never been able to explain flying off into the wild blue yonder, no matter how much Cîroc they drank. Thankfully, he was able to loan me his helicopter for the night. This had better be good," Viktoria said, her tone tight and clipped.

"Counselors, please forgive my abrupt request and the lateness of the hour. I believe Mael explained during his call that this is a matter of grave importance. A friend of mine and I were nearly blown up by an unknown assailant. We believe it is in connection with several disappearances of vampire females."

"And why should we intervene in this matter? Were they hunted or just asking for trouble? Perhaps this is a war between rivals. And as such, we have no authority to intervene." Tarik leaned forward, an elegant hand resting on the table, cold aquamarine eyes enough to make a weaker male shudder.

"The females who have gone missing appear to be civilians. It is a danger to all of us if hunters have resumed activity. It is even worse if there is an unsanctioned war between races. Were it not something that has occurred in the past, I would not even consider, but we have two of the last-known locations of the missing females, and I seek access to nearby traffic cams and any cellular device footage near their location and my own from last evening. I would also like to see information on any grievances filed against local clans in your jurisdiction, Viktoria."

"Oh? Well, that is a mighty bold request. It's one thing to surveil humans, but quite another to hack into one of our constituent's personal information. Vampire locations are not revealed to anyone, let alone me, considering certain vulnerabilities." While Viktoria was speaking in riddles, everyone at the table knew she was referring to their sensitivities to UV rays.

"I would not presume to ask such a thing, *madame,* were it not for the safety of so many who are under your protection as their representative." The formality of the Order, when they were some of the most cutthroat of each of the races, was galling. Each of them had declared war against the others and secretly plotted to gain power, prestige, and in some instances, fame through any manner of dishonorable methods.

She fingered the quarter-sized deep brown stones at her neck. She was a pale woman with icy blond hair. She had been an assassin and double agent during WWI, found shot and left for dead in Iceland, turned by Lago. When he met an untimely death, she slithered her way up the Vampire food chain until she landed at the top.

"I am seeking access to a local vampire business."

Her brow quirked, the corners of her mouth turning up at the ends. "Is that so, Anwar? I can't imagine why..."

"I am attempting to determine whether Farr—I mean, the owner's records have been compromised." While some of the Order members had not shown any malice to Anwar and his father, he still couldn't trust them. There was no way he would reveal how much Farrah had come to mean to him.

"If we grant you this access, should we find that the source is immortal, will you allow us to assign the appropriate punishment to the perpetrator?" Haster queried. He had not acquired a new body since the last time Anwar had seen him. Uncommon for demons, who often enjoyed occupying new humans. How they'd managed to slip that deal into the accords was beyond him. Thankfully.

"Of course. If it is human, however, I would ask for immediate execution of the perpetrator, following interrogation," Anwar replied. Guess he couldn't blame Haster for the ask. The numbers mattered to every race. Which was the reason he'd sought out Farrah's services in the first place. Dwindling numbers could cost valuable currency of power. No one wanted to deal with that.

A knock on the marble table brought Anwar's attention far right. "Anything else you would like to share with us in order to help us execute an emergency order, Anwar?" Zaria said. She was a peaceful soul, most of the time. Tonight, her eyes were the same sepia coloring of her skin. She used shifting as if it were makeup, changing her appearance as the mood suited her.

"No, there is no more to share at this time."

"And we cannot assume you'll be on your own. Who will accompany you on your mission?" Viktoria, still smirking, was bound and determined to not let him off easy, it seemed.

"Maelstrom. He awaits my return in the atrium, ma'am." When he wasn't seated at the Order, he was required to address the Order members appropriately. This requirement did not stop it from chaffing his ass.

"All right." Viktoria looked up and down the table in the torchlit space. "Shall we dismiss Anwar so we may deliberate, barring any further questions from the members?"

A chorus of agreement rose from each seat in various forms of ayes, yesses, and um-hmms.

"I will await your decision in the corridor." With a short bow, Anwar excused himself and left the room. It was no surprise that he walked out frustrated. They were no more than power-hungry figureheads, never offering to lift one finger to make the lives of those they represented better. Every meeting was a fashion show, an elegant distraction from things of significant import. He wanted to liberate their heads from their shoulders, but their existence was representative of Constantine's life work. And also, protection of their race from those who would seek to destroy them in order to gain the Atlanteans' most prized possessions. As far as Anwar was concerned, it was a pile of scrap metal and meaningless stones at the bottom of the sea. But as the last true prince of Atlantis, he was just doing his job.

"The regents in there *regenting*?" Mael chortled.

Anwar leaned against the golden calf Haster had stolen and was hiding from the archangels. It was probably only a matter of time before they found it. Probably pissed Mael off to no end. If it did, he had never let on. "Yeah, they're doing something. You know how they roll."

"Indeed. You don't suppose any of them had anything to do with it, do you?" Mael's question had been unspoken and hovering on the ride over and as they'd waited to be admitted. Neither of them had voiced it.

Even Haster had thought about it, as evil as he was. "I can't be sure. But there is a stipulation if I find out it's an immortal who is behind it."

"Yeah?"

"Um-hmm. If so, I am to bring them before the Order. Take absolutely no action."

"If you don't mind my saying so, that is complete and utter bullshit."

"What choice did I have but to agree?"

Mael paced around, hand on his chin and pondering, like he always did when looking for a loophole. "I guess we'll cross that bridge when we come to it." He had changed from his normal bespoke suit into something a little more incognito. He wore black cargo pants, most likely laden with weapons of some sort, a vest, and a long-sleeved military-grade flak jacket. Anwar never bothered to ask where he got all that shit.

Fallen angels kept nearly as much of their powers as they had in Heaven. Their punishment was the denial of access to the pearly gates. It was the reason Haster's boss was so angry. And most likely the source of Mael's snark.

"Looks like it," Anwar said on a frustrated breath.

"You think your female stayed put like you asked?" Mael leaned against the wall opposite the double doors.

"First, she says she's not my female. Second, I don't believe she is the type to listen well. But, hopefully, we'll get to whoever is responsible before she does. And if Leila is with her, I don't even want to think about what might have happened."

While Anwar chuckled a bit, Mael did not. "Leila is quite a female," Mael murmured.

"She did a number on you, didn't she?"

"No, she was..." Mael stared off into space for a moment in a way that made Anwar feel like an intruder. When he came back from wherever he'd drifted off to, he seemed as if he'd left a piece of himself there. "I was the asshole. I abandoned her to go aid my brother, Azazel. In the end, he was the reason I fell. Just goes to show, I should have followed my heart. While I still would have ended up in the same place, at least I would have had her in my life. And it would have been worth it."

Anwar didn't have much to say in response. To disagree would be a lie, and to agree would only add salt to the wound. "We live and learn, Mael."

"I guess we do. Damn, are they going to take all day?" He was changing the subject.

"Probably, if only to piss me off more."

"Must be payback for all the times you disagreed with them." Mael took a seat on the floor, not going anywhere near the calf. "I am willing to bet they'll say yes. Something isn't right with Viktoria. I know it. When I called her, she was too eager to convene."

"All due respect, brother, I know Viktoria better than you. She is only in a hurry to make other people miserable. If anything, she just wanted to get me to groveling level."

Mael went silent again, and before Anwar could inquire, the door flew open and Viktoria stepped out into the hallway. Both Anwar and Mael stood in her presence and awaited the decision.

"We've made our choice, Anwar. Your request is granted. We would like a full report on what occurred and who... if there are any survivors, should you find the females."

To say he was relieved was an understatement. There'd been no bodies, so he presumed the females had been taken. Not murdered. Whoever it was had tried to take Farrah—and possibly Anwar himself—out of commission for good. He needed to stop them before they succeeded. "Thank you, Viktoria. Do they need to see me before I go?"

"No. Just go with our blessing."

She wasn't like herself. Something about her was off, and it didn't seem to be just Anwar who thought so. Mael was looking at her through squinted eyes. "Is something wrong?" Mael asked.

"It's just that... someone I care about, one of my children, hasn't been heard from in a few weeks. I thought she was just blowing off steam, but now that you bring this to our attention, it has been a while. We'd had a disagreement, you see." Her green eyes glossed over, and there was genuine sadness and concern in them. Something Anwar had never seen in her.

"What's her name?" Anwar asked.

"Sarielle. She is my height, has long dark braids, and usually wears red lipstick. That probably sounds like nearly every vampire, but I have a picture on my cell. I'll text it to you." There was something close to pleading in her voice.

"If you thought she was missing, why haven't you gone looking for her?"

"Well, in most every vampire life, there is a crisis of sorts. A time when they become a little afraid of immortality. Of spending years on the planet without having any real sense of purpose. In her case, she's young and wanted to mate a male she barely knew. I suggested she rethink it, given the power displacement. She disagreed. I guess I just thought she would get over it." She swiped at an errant tear that streamed down her face. "Dammit, Anwar. Just do what you have to do." In an instant, her normal look of derision spread over her face, replacing any moment of sadness or fear.

"I intend to. I will report back once I hear anything."

"The office in downtown Detroit will have all the information. I'm sending you the passwords and the location. I have it moved every few years. This time, it's inside the Main Library. The vaults are in the basement." Viktoria pressed a key into his hand and, with a nod, turned and walked in the opposite direction of the chambers. He couldn't really blame her. There was nothing worse than dealing with others in times of great sorrow or anguish.

While Anwar didn't really know what she was going through, he didn't want to find out. There was nothing that would stop him from saving Farrah from whoever seemed to be targeting her. First it was her clients, then a car she was in gets blown up? Someone sure seemed to have a hard-on for her. If it was the last thing he did, he would find them and make them pay.

## CHAPTER TWENTY

*MAEL*

Despite everything happening around Mael, his head was not in the game. His mind was back at Anwar's apartment, focused with laser-like precision on Leila. She'd been so very angry.

"You good?"

Anwar's voice cut into Mael's thoughts, and as he came back online, he realized he'd been trapped in his own worries for the entirety of the return trip. They were pulling into the parking lot of Detroit's Main Library. "Yeah, just a little tired."

"Um, I hate to break the news to you, pal, but angels don't sleep."

"I meant in my soul. You ever wonder what would have happened if you'd made different choices in your lifetime?"

"Sometimes," Anwar replied, steering the Jeep into a parking space. "I do. But the best part of having no real expiration date is having time to fix whatever you've fucked up. C'mon. Let's get in here."

Mael didn't say anything, but in his heart, he knew he would never be able to make it up to Leila. She wasn't the type who was big on forgiveness.

Following Anwar into the building, he noticed all the lights were off. It was late for humans, so it made sense, but he wondered if there were any tricky alarm systems or anything preventing access to the structure. His concerns were assuaged, however, as Anwar shifted the metal plate on the face of the lock around and inserted the key Viktoria had given him.

Things opened up with one turn, and a trail of blue lights leading down the main hallway with an illuminated red arrow pointing around a corner lit up. "Talk about a welcome wagon," Mael said, walking through the door Anwar held open for him.

"Yeah, you know how connected the Order is to politicians. Hell, this building was probably built with Order funds back in eighteen sixty-whatever-the-fuck." He turned and hit the lock from the inside before walking to Mael's side.

"All right, let's do this."

"Yeah, I'm texting Farrah to let her know to sit tight." After tapping out a message to the cell he'd left with her, he went to put it in his pocket, but within seconds, a text came back. "Hmmm..."

"What is it?"

"She sent back 'K.'"

"That's it?"

"Yup," he said.

"You know she's still pissed, right?"

"I don't doubt it."

"What are you going to do about it?"

"I think we'll have to just see where it takes us." The pair started walking down the hallway. When they reached the arrow, they went left. Somewhere near the center of the wide-open space was another bright-red, pulsing arrow. "You think she'll forgive me?" he finally asked.

"Since you're convinced of your sexual prowess—"

"Pretty sure that's not the answer, my guy."

With a shrug, Mael started down the stairs. "Take my advice or not, but it'll be grand gesture time after this mess. You can bank on that."

"Yeah well, it's up to her. No matter what I do, she has the upper hand."

"That's always the case with females." Mael's groan echoed in the hallway.

When they descended the stairs, there was a second row of lights, this time, fluorescent. Inside another room, then through a passageway, they reached the door with a lock on it. Anwar quickly afforded them access, then they went inside to find walls with flat-screen smartboards and five neatly lined desks, each with a top-of-the-line MacBook atop it. Anwar pulled out his phone again while walking over to the desk in the front of the room. "Viktoria sent me the network info and passwords. Shouldn't take us too long to find whatever we need."

"All right, give it to me. I'll help," Mael said, taking the desk next to Anwar.

Within a few clicks, Anwar was in. He then passed the phone over to Mael.

The system came on with a low-grade hum, and they were off and running. Mael started with the traffic cameras, locating the previous night's footage. The Tabernacle was under St. Mary's church downtown, in what would have been the cellar. Fitting for a vampire night-club, perfect for hiding their dirty deeds.

After locating the Greektown camera on the corner of Lafayette and St. Antione, Mael went to the time of the explosion. The moment he got to 4:13 a.m., he saw the blinding flash. Backing it up an hour, he found two men in the grainy images approaching Anwar's car and climbing under it. "I think I've got something."

Anwar leaned over and stared at the screen. "I can't make anything out."

"Yeah, but your car is parked near the camera, and I believe that's the only way out. Let me see if they get into a car." Another few minutes passed by, and bingo. "A Lincoln Navigator, dark-colored, although..." Mael leaned closer to the screen. "I can't make out the license plate, but since no one else came in or out of the Tabernacle during that time, pretty sure that's their car. Flossy fucks. Why would they pick such a high-profile car if they needed to be incognito?"

"Most likely humans."

For a moment, Mael thought of whether or not saving the missing females would help Leila to see him in a different light. Chances on that were slim, but he still wanted to help.

"Okay. Let's see if we can get more off this one." Mael scooted over and watched as Anwar navigated the recording.

Scrolling through the last couple of weeks seemed to take hours, but it probably was only a few minutes. "You know," Anwar said, "I'm going to tell Farrah about my past. I mean, about who I am. All of it."

Mael was stunned for a moment. There had never

been one time in the history of their relationship that Anwar had ever wanted to share his past with a female. While Anwar mating Farrah was exactly what Viktoria wanted so she could banish him and his father from the Order once and for all, he was happy for his friend. While Mael had been condemned to servitude to Constantine, he and Anwar had become as close as brothers. And Con had treated him like a son, despite the fact they weren't the same race. They were family, and if Anwar was finally getting close to someone, Mael welcomed his happiness. "I think you should tell her."

"I just don't want to hide anything from her. You can't trust someone who would purposefully lie or withhold information. I'm not that male. I need her to know who I am. And there's no way I would violate her trust. I want someone who I can share everything with."

Mael thought on that for a moment. Trust. He was violating the very thing Anwar required in all of his relationships. They were brothers, after all. One day, he would tell him how Viktoria had blackmailed him. And it would happen soon. He wouldn't be able to live with it for much longer, and he hated being a backstabbing bastard. "You're right, Anwar."

"You said it was a Navigator?"

"Yup." He leaned in and watched the truck pull up next to a female walking away from the crowd. A cloaked figure hopped out, grabbed her, and yanked her into the car. There was no way a human could have done that to a supernatural... "Freeze it, Anwar."

When he did, Mael committed the thankfully clearer image of the license plate to memory. Why they still couldn't tell whether the males were immortals, they certainly had another piece to go on. He went back to his system and found the Detroit Police sigil on the desktop. "I figured the Order had their hands everywhere."

"Me too." Anwar was still at his system, probably looking for more on the disappearances.

"Got 'em. The car is registered to a Billy McDermott. It's a business." Tapping into Google Earth, he put in the address and found an abandoned building. "It's the Packard Plant. That old demo." Mael closed down the map and went to search for McDermott in the police portal, then the city's treasury department by the address of the building. "It says here he was supposed to convert that old heap into condos over five years ago. Never did anything with it."

"It's late. You think he's there tonight?"

"Maybe, but I found his home address. Let's head to the plant first, then swing by his house. Wherever he is, we'll find him."

"Bet." Anwar began shutting his system down.

As they walked out, Mael clapped Anwar on the shoulder. "You know, I hope you and Farrah can make a go of it. She's good for you. You aren't nearly as big of a dick as you were before you met her."

"Well, thanks... I think. Asshole."

Heading up the stairs, Mael thought of what he would say when the time came to tell the truth about how Viktoria had learned of Lelania's power and then blackmailed him into betraying Anwar. Yet another bridge he'd have to cross when the time came.

## CHAPTER TWENTY-ONE

Leila, although silent for the majority of the ride to the abandoned warehouse, was efficient. They'd taken her Hellcat and made it there within ten minutes of leaving Melody and raiding Mike's locker. As promised, they'd gained guns, which would help if Ennis was right about the kidnappers being humans. If they were immortals, that would be a whole other ball of wax to deal with.

While Farrah wanted to talk to Leila about their blow-up, there would probably be plenty of time later. Besides, where they were going, she didn't want or need to be distracted.

Farrah put her phone down after texting Anwar a single letter in reply. He'd asked her to sit tight. She'd said "K." The best alternative to a lie was an omission. While it wouldn't fly with her, and she was sure he would be mad too if he ever found out, these were her friends and clients. She didn't want some knight in shining armor swooping in for her. Surely, she could protect herself from humans. And most immortals would be no match for

Leila's strength, given her age. She was a liberated female. She would save the day if needed.

"This it?" Farrah asked, breaking what felt like hours of silence between them.

"Looks like." Leila navigated the car over the roughshod parking surface and came to a stop at the boarded-up entrance to the building. "Well, let's go see this Billy guy. From the looks of this place, I'm glad to have a couple guns. And if you need to use it, remember to shoot first. Got it?"

She didn't wait for an answer. Instead, she got out and started walking to the entryway. Farrah jumped out and nearly rolled an ankle as she stepped on a broken piece of concrete. "Wait up," she cried, a tinge of pain shooting through her bone. When Leila didn't slow down, Farrah turned up the heat and used a bit of her vampire ability to catch up. She sped past Leila and bent down to start yanking the board free of the wall. Whoever had put it up hadn't spared a single nail because it took several yanks before it came free.

Once it was down, she pulled the glass door and found it unlocked. "After you, madame," she said, giving Leila an exaggerated wave inside.

With a roll of her eyes, Leila walked by and into the darkened corridor. It was pitch black, and the stench of rats and decay hung thick in the air, along with what must have been ten years of dust. The deeper they went inside, the ghastlier it became.

With every step, Farrah scanned the debris-filled hallway to ensure nothing or no one caught them unaware. Leila was just in front of her, so she was probably doing the same.

As they came to another corridor, she could see a

wide-open space in front of them that had collapsed in on itself. She wondered for a moment whether, given the condition of the building, vampires could survive in such a place. Long ago, they would've lived underground during the daytime to prevent being burned to death in their sleep from the rising sun. With technological advances also came a bit of safety from their natural weaknesses. Along with it also came other challenges, but ultimately, they were better off. With only a few hours before sunrise, she certainly hoped they wouldn't have to find out.

Behind them, something shattered, like glass meeting concrete at a thousand miles per hour. "Leila," she whispered, then turned around.

A loud *thud* sounded out, and she heard something hit the ground. Turning again, she was met with a kaleidoscope of pain and brilliant stars in her vision right before everything went black.

CHAPTER TWENTY-TWO

"So... pulling up to an abandoned building with the doors wide open is a little too convenient, isn't it Mael?" Anwar looked from the sweet-ass, abandoned automobile to the dilapidated property that might as well have had a welcome mat out.

"I think so. What do you say we turn around, park on the street, and find some other way into the joint?" Mael was leaning forward, his eyes gazing up to the overhead balustrade. It looked like an old walkway from one part of the factory to the other. "We can walk around the building first. Since there's a car out there though, I'd say someone is home."

"Yup." Anwar killed his lights and backed out until he was on the street in front of the building. He and Mael hopped out of the car and sprinted around the building. On the second turn around, Mael tapped him on the shoulder.

"I'm going to head up high for a second."

"All right. Yell if you see something," he said.

"Copy that."

A strong breeze blew around Anwar's locs as Mael flew past him. In another second, as Anwar walked close to the building and kicked at basement windows, he heard the sound of flapping wings.

He looked up to find a shirtless Mael with broad, black wings lifting him high into the sky as he soared over the building and finally out of sight. Mael's wings were tipped with iron, so flying wasn't something he normally did. Only when it was necessary.

"Showoff." Anwar continued on his trek down the row of caged and boarded windows. While he couldn't see anything inside, he imagined they would need some light if they were human. Big *if* there. A part of him was afraid it was one of the other races preying on the vampires who held all the numbers.

They were the most powerful, given their massive citizenship, and for obvious reasons, were careful with their locations. Since the hunters were gone, the races had become a little less likely to roam from place to place, finally able to settle down in some areas, blending into the periphery of countless humans in urban centers.

Anwar reached the end of one side of the massive compound and turned down the backside of the building. Overgrown grass in its recesses made his pathway a little less than ideal, but at least those windows were absent their boards. He didn't see anything yet, but one of the windows had a bent frame. He drew closer and peered in, ensuring there wasn't anyone there to surprise him if he went in that way.

Wind hit him just as he leaned in, and Anwar jumped backward, turned, and caught the bastard at his throat.

"It's me..." the voice choked out.

"Mael, don't fucking do that. I could have ended you."
Anwar released him, muttering curses.

"I doubt you could have ended me, given I'm an angel. But, I'm pretty sure you dislocated my esophagus."

"Next time whistle or something."

"Yeah, I'll remember that for our next ops mission. There's nothing overhead. In fact, half the ceiling is caved in. Probably nobody up top. We'd better go in down here."

"Yup. This looks like the best entry point." Stepping forward, Anwar pulled at some of the tall grass to clear a path, then yanked the bent wire from the wall.

Fortunately, the window was unlocked, but it was rusted shut. It took a bit more to shimmy it open, but finally, it came free.

He looked back at Mael, who was still shirtless and fully winged. "You gonna be able to get those bitches through here?"

"Don't you worry about me." In the blink of an eye, Mael faded into the ether.

Anwar cursed again only to turn around and find the bastard smiling up at him from the open window. "Need a hand?"

"If you don't back your ass up. And if you could have gone in that whole time, why the hell didn't you?"

"Iron. We can't get in through there. All races have weaknesses. Remember?"

"Whatever. Coming in." Anwar grabbed the sill and hauled himself inside. The room stank of sewage, and the air was stale. Fighting against his roiling stomach, he inhaled to see if he could scent anyone in the building. The stench was too dense to smell anything other than rot.

Mael walked over to the door and tried it. The hinges screamed as he pulled them open. Anwar waited to see if he'd found something. He waved him to his side.

"What?" When Mael pointed down the hallway, Anwar stuck his head out.

Down at the end, there was a flickering light, and he could faintly hear shuffling noises.

The pair of them, after motioning to one another, crouched to the floor and made their way toward the shimmering shaft of light. After what seemed like an eternity, they made it to the entryway. The door was open, but there was a corner just inside, and he couldn't see whether anyone was inside.

Mael rose to his full height and dimmed out. Anwar was sure he would never get used to that shit. Of course, they had never been in a situation where Mael needed to use his angel powers. They had all enjoyed a pretty relaxed existence until the last few days had changed their lives forever. He'd never imagined he would have been breaking into an abandoned building to take out someone who'd caused someone he could be falling for pain.

Before he could delve into the suddenness of his emotions, he heard something crackle, like bones breaking.

"What the fuck," was heard next in a man's voice, immediately followed by gunfire.

Without thinking, he charged into the room and headed for the first body he saw. They smelled of humans, and for a moment, he thanked Mael's boss that he wouldn't have to deal with the Order, nor really think about his actions.

Anwar was on top of the first human in seconds. The

balding male had a thick neck and an even thicker midsection. He sank his fingers into pale, fleshy skin that reddened more and more the harder he squeezed. He didn't even see a man—all he saw was a monster.

"Get off him," he heard from behind him as a set of hands grabbed at his shoulders.

A familiar gust of wind came, then the hands were gone and Anwar knew Mael had taken him out.

"Anwar, there isn't anyone else here. We need to find out what he knows."

Despite understanding perfectly what Mael meant and what it would mean if he choked the life out of the degenerate he was straddling, they may never find out what had happened. Reluctantly, he freed him.

Asshole number two rolled onto his side and coughed, struggling to get air into his undeserving lungs.

Mael snatched him up from the floor, and Anwar stepped back as he dragged him to the only chair left upright in the room. It was all he could do not to go after him again, but Mael had been sensible, and he needed the cooler head to prevail.

"Where are they?"

"I ain't telling you shit, freak. You might as well kill me now." He was a white man with shaggy, unremarkable brown hair. The markings of age and abuse were etched in his skin. He was probably fifty human years and didn't look athletic in the least.

"Wrong answer." Holding him by a dingy T-shirt, Mael punched him square in the face.

"Fuck you," the human said, spitting out blood that dribbled over Mael's fists.

"You're the one that's going to be fucked if you don't

tell me where the females are," Anwar said, stepping forward and going after his neck again.

It took a few seconds for Mael to get him off the guy. "Hey, hey, I've got this," he said, pushing him back with a massive show of strength.

Once he was done, he returned to the man who had a sudden glimmer of fear in his eyes. It only took one glance to understand why. Mael had released his wings, which spanned the length of the room. They were huge up close and, for a human, probably caused him to defecate immediately. From the smell of things, Anwar wasn't far off in his assumption.

"Are you and your friends responsible for the disappearance of the females?" Mael's voice was deathly serious, and all the previous bravado was stripped from his target.

"We just did as we were told."

"Who? Who told you to do it?"

"Don't know. Somebody called our boss, Billy, offered him some money, and told us to nab the girls. They gave us water with silver flecks in it and told us where they would be. Uploaded pics to our cell phones," he said, wheezing with every breath he took. "I need—I need my inhaler."

Anwar surged again, incensed at his audacity to ask for anything when he'd been part of kidnapping and probably torturing females. "Fuck your needs, bitch. Where are they?"

"I gotta take you to them. And I will, just need my inhaler."

"All right, where the hell is it," Mael spat out.

"Pocket. My front pocket," he said.

Mael took a step back, releasing the germ's collar. His

hand immediately went to his pants pocket, and he extracted a cylindrical tube. He brought it to his mouth and simultaneously squeezed and puffed until he was breathing with some semblance of normalcy.

"Now, where are they?"

"Down the hall. Tanner has the key," he said, still a bit wheezy.

"Where is this Tanner?" Anwar was a hair off the bastard's ass. It was taking everything inside him to keep him from killing the guy.

"I think he's dead." He pointed to the male on the floor closest to Anwar. He lay in a heap, neck bent in a position that was most assuredly indicative of death.

Anwar bent down and rifled through the dead guy's pockets until he found a set of keys. Bringing them back, he handed them to Mael.

"All right, let's move," Mael barked.

The human stood up, and the moment his ass left the seat, Mael had a hand around the back of his neck. "It's this way." Shuffling forward, he headed into the hallway and to the left. The hall was darkened still, but Mael and Anwar didn't need light to find their way.

The leader, however, stumbled and tripped. Each time, Mael hoisted him up by his throat before he hit the ground.

"What was the reason they were taking the females?" Mael asked, continuing the line of questioning as they went along.

"Something about the immortals creating a weapon. Some prophecy or whatever. Look, I didn't believe 'em in the first place. They paid me a couple grand a week to sit in this hole and keep an eye on them at night. Told us nobody was needed in the daytime. They knocked 'em down, and I set 'em up. We had about eight until tonight. They took two of them somewhere. That's when these other two showed up. Just walked into the place."

"Other two," Anwar said. The first thing that popped into his mind was Farrah and her one-word fucking text. If she was in there, so help him, he was going to rip out that guy's spleen.

"Who blew up the car?"

"Wasn't us," he choked out, his voice growing raspier the harder Mael squeezed. "We were just on the girls. That's it. I swear it… but there's more than what we do here. Way bigger than just us. I can give you the number they contact us from."

Mael glanced over his shoulder at Anwar, a grim look in his eyes. "Give me your phone."

"Here…" The human took a cell that looked like a burner and handed it to Mael.

Mael passed the phone to Anwar and returned his attention to the poor bastard who may not have known he only had seconds left to live. As chill as Mael could be at times, he was an archangel and would rip the human to shreds given the chance. "Go faster," Mael growled, more animal than male.

Anwar could hear the man shuffling faster, and finally, they reached the end of a long passageway.

Obviously nervous, the visibly nervous human's hands shook so badly the keys jingled. Sticking one in and turning a lock that sounded ancient, he stepped into the darkened silence. In another second, screams came through the doorway. Hands reaching out of the darkness grabbed him and wrestled him to the ground. The shrieks were savage and unholy.

Mael jumped, and Anwar felt an arm go across his

chest, holding him back. "Goddammit," he cursed and waited for a moment before attempting to see inside.

When he peered in, he could see five females on top of their jailer. Blood was squirting from freshly gouged wounds as one female after another took a bite from him, chunks of flesh strewn into the air.

"Farrah," he called into the room. Some of the yelling stopped, only a few of them screaming then. "Farrah, are you in here?" He hoped there wasn't another room. If she was there, he prayed she was accounted for in the melee. Alive. Well.

Someone rose from the pileup and began walking in his direction. Despite her being covered in blood, hair everywhere, Anwar knew it was Farrah. Before she could take another step, he ran to her, lifting her up and cradling her in his arms. "Are you hurt? Are you okay, Farrah?"

"I—I think so. Did you find any other girls? I'm looking for Ei..." She hesitated in what sounded like a hiccup. "Another client could be here."

"I don't think there were any other holding cells here. Mael was pretty thorough."

"What about those bastards? Was he the only one?" Her eyes were wide, and he could hear the rapid pulse of her heart, feel it against his chest as he pulled her close.

"No, there were more. And maybe even some we didn't get, but you're safe now. I'll never let anyone harm you again. Don't you worry about that."

"Anwar," Mael said, sidling up to him, "just being honest, from the looks of that guy, I think they'll do okay without us."

Anwar glanced over at what was left of the male. He was in shreds, and above him stood a tattered Leila, staring down at him as he took his last breath, a sardonic smile on her lips.

"C'mon. We'll get you all home," Anwar said.

"I'm coming with you, though," Farrah said in a whisper.

"Are you sure? I know one of these females is like a sister to you, so I underst—"

"No. I'm coming with you, Anwar. I can't be alone tonight."

He looked down into her eyes and knew what she meant. Of course, he would have respected her wishes, but there wasn't a single part of him that didn't want her tucked safely in his arms. "Okay, baby. Whatever you need," he said. "Whatever you need."

# CHAPTER TWENTY-THREE

Farrah rolled around in Anwar's arms, laying the VMA phone on the small table near the oversized bed they languished in. She would have to remember to replace her own soon. Thankfully, Eire knew the phone number, as well. While Farrah was cognizant of Eire's request for privacy, and taking a call from her could be risky to her identity, Farrah needed to be sure she was safe. If she didn't turn up soon, Farrah knew she would have to tell Anwar. Or worse, Eire's father. She hadn't been in the old factory where they'd been held, but she also hadn't returned any calls or texts. Even if she wanted to remain anonymous, safety would have to come first.

Anwar kissed her along her neck, slow and deliberate. He hadn't let her go after bathing, then feeding her, ensuring she was taken care of, finally tucking her in beside him just as the sun rose over the Detroit River. His blackout shades came down as his penthouse went into daylight protection phase.

"Thank you for coming for me," she whispered into

his hair as she lay across his chest. They would still have to deal with the fact that he'd lied to her, but after nearly dying several times, it was something she wanted to tackle another day. She needed to figure things out, but he'd risked his life for her, and somehow, they would have to map out the way forward. But she wanted to do it with him at her side.

"I'll always look for you, Farrah. No matter where you are, what I have to do. I'll find you. Now and forever. Although, based on what you've told me, I think you were going to be okay if I hadn't."

"Those poor females. Some of them had been there for weeks. The saddest thing is they never once tried to escape. I think it was the silver shards they'd tortured them with. It must have been what they hit Leila and me with when we arrived."

"Yeah, Mael found some silver-plated brass knuckles. I'm just glad we got there when we did." Anwar ran his fingers through her damp hair, still wet from the bath he'd given her.

"Me too." She lifted her head and kissed him on his shoulder. The one with the tats. "I do love these," she said, kissing them again.

Anwar shifted, taking a hand in his. "I'm glad you like them," he said, soft lips pressed against her fingers. "But, I'm afraid this isn't over, Farrah. Did you happen to hear about the two other females?"

She couldn't help the sigh. All Farrah wanted was to push the events out of her mind. But Eire wasn't in the cell. When she'd asked about the females, the news wasn't great. "No one knew who the person was, but when he got there, he took them. But all my clients were in that room. Except…

well, one that I fear is still missing. Do you think..." She hesitated before diving into the very thing that could mean the end of her. "Would the Order help find them?"

Anwar frowned. "I think we'll have to involve them at some point. But Mael is working on something. He got a phone off one of the men at the warehouse. We'll track down that lead. The Order will be our last resort."

She felt a little better, but worry still lingered. The Order, while they had helped Anwar, was still a threat to her clients and other people she loved. Especially Leila. She'd warned her about the dangers of opening the agency from the start. And now, her fears had come to fruition. "Okay," she said.

For a moment, Anwar stilled beneath her, his hand stopping mid-stroke in her hair. "I've been meaning to talk to you about something."

Oh, hell. Their relationship was tenuous at best. She was afraid whatever he was about to say would blow her little resolution to deal with things as they came to smithereens. Just when she thought she was in control of her life and destiny, Anwar was about to turn into a frog. *Fuck...* "Right, I mean, it's none of my business. So if you'd prefer to keep it light—"

"No. I need to tell you something, and it may come as a shock. I wanted to tell you the night of the explosion, but everything kind of went haywire on us, so... this is my chance, and I'm going to take it."

Farrah sat up on the bed, using the cover to provide a type of barrier between her and whatever he was about to reveal to her. "Okay... I'm not going to lie. I kind of feel like I need to brace myself for what's coming next." Anwar didn't change his grave expression. She knew he was about to tell her something that would shake her to her core.

"I was trying to tell you before. I'm uh... well, I'm not what you think I am."

"Oh..." *Maybe he was mated already?*

"No. You see..." He stammered, then looked down at his hands. "I'm not a vampire."

She let out a long breath. Hadn't she seen fangs? Well, no because he'd never actually fed from her. "I don't understand. You told me you don't need to feed often because you're older. If you aren't a vampire, then what are you?"

"I'm Atlantean."

"Like from Georgia? Because I'm Southern too, originally."

"No, I mean... I'm one of the survivors from Atlantis." He looked at her with tired eyes, as if he hadn't slept in a million years. "There were only sixteen of us who survived. Before our city fell, we were the closest thing to gods on earth. But, our arrogance led us to be cursed by a witch. Her magic was so powerful she crumbled the streets from beneath our feet. And all who survived have to feed on the blood of humans or vampires once a month. But that's not all."

"Waaait a minute, Anwar. This is too fast. First, you're a member of the Order..."

"My father is, not me."

"Yes, but technically. And now you're not even a vampire."

"Well... shit. How do I say this without freaking you out?"

"Go ahead. I'm already pretty freaked."

"We are the reason vampires exist."

"So... you and your people created vampires?" Her heart beat at her temples as she processed Anwar's news.

"Not us, per se. It was the result of the spell. This witch used dark magic. That is the reason for vampires. We were just the conduits. Ultimately, yes, all vampires are, in some way or another, infected with our original curse. It's why I needed to tell you before... well, if we were to be mated."

For a moment, Farrah felt as if she were about to float away from there. She swayed a bit as the gravity of what he was saying washed over her. "I'm missing something, aren't I?"

"Well... all vampires feel at least a little subservient to us, and they don't know why. That is, until I met you. You were the first to ever challenge me. To resist me. There is something"—he inhaled deeply—"magical about you, Farrah Grant. I don't know what it is, or why, but you are the first female I've ever been with that didn't leave me wondering whether it was me she liked or if it was the effect of the curse."

"What about other races? Does it happen with, say, shifters, or the fae?"

He blushed and turned away from her. "I've uh... I've only been with three females... all vampires."

"Um... are you over two thousand years old?"

"I am."

She pondered him for a moment. Three females in two thousand years. Farrah was only about fifty in human years, and she'd been with three males in the last five years. "Oh... okay."

"I know that may seem like a lot. There must be at least sixteen Atlanteans to keep our council seat. When one of us died last year, it fell to me to become mated.

That's the other thing. I know how you feel about the Order, but if we mate during my father's rest period, I will have to deal with them."

"I mean, you do come with some baggage, don't you?"

Anwar sat up and turned his back to her. She could see the tension as the muscles in his back flexed. "I do. And I will understand if you don't want any part of this."

"Anwar," she said.

"It's a lot to ask anyone. I'm not even your same species. And I didn't tell you before we had sex. Hell, I didn't even tell you I was attached to the Order. It's too much for me to ask you to forgive me."

"Forgive you? Anwar, look at me."

Slowly, he shifted on the bed. Resting a hand on his glorious muscles and the intricate circles etched into his umber skin, she waited for him to face her. When he did, she could see the tears falling and wondered how she had been so lucky to meet a male as fine as he was and with such a wonderful heart. He didn't say anything when he looked into her eyes, but then again, he didn't need to.

"It's not about who your family is. And if you would have told me the truth about the Order before, we would have worked through it. I'm still wrapping my head around all those things. We have a lot to do to build trust with one another. But if you can be open with me, I think we can give it a shot."

Anwar leaned forward and placed a gentle kiss on her shoulder. "I can do that. I.... I've never had anyone to share all my dark secrets with, and I'm far from perfect. But I'm willing to do everything in my power to be the male you need me to be. I'm willing to be perfect for you."

Farrah shook her head and laid a hand on his in the mess of covers. "I wasn't looking for the perfect vampire male. In fact, I may have been looking for love when I started the VMA, but since then, I have found my own kind of happiness. So you may not be a vampire, but I don't think you have any influence over me. Especially since you asked me to stay put and I still went looking for Billy McDermott. So, whatever fears you have over me not wanting you because of your race, I'm here to tell you, that is not me. I don't care who you are or where you came from. The only thing that matters is that you love me with a full heart, the way... the way I care about you. And maybe we aren't mated just yet, but I am enjoying the ride."

"So, you want to try this with me? At least for a little while?" His eyes warmed as he watched her.

On bended knees, she stared deeply into his eyes before allowing the oversized robe he lent her to slide from her shoulders. "I'm willing to stay on the ride, and we'll figure it all out whenever we get there."

Anwar rose up and pulled her close to him as they faced one another on the bed. Running a hand between her thighs, he teased her clit with a talented forefinger.

Her thighs shook, but he slipped his arm inside the robe and around her waist, holding her tight as he explored her. "My turn," he whispered, licking her neck before he sank fangs into her skin. From the way he exposed his neck to her, as if in surrender... It seemed he wanted her to take his blood too.

A flash of heat tinged with ecstasy ran the length of her body. She had never felt such a deep puncture, and his draw felt as if it were pulling directly from her core. She rode his fingers, holding his wrist in place until she was near orgasmic. She allowed her fangs to graze his neck but shrank away before she could strike. Blood-mating was too much to consider while distracted by lust.

Farrah's breasts drew into tight beads as rivulets of blood trickled down the front of her body. The intensity of his thrusts had almost taken her to the edge, almost driven her over, when he pulled away from her, and she cried out as she felt his absence in her soul. "Don't..."

"Don't worry. I plan on taking my time on you," he said, his voice a rough demand that made her shiver.

He laid her back onto the bed, and she opened her legs before him. With eager fingers, she spread herself, inviting him to taste. Hungry eyes roved over her right before he bent down and ran his tongue down her body, blazing a heated sensual path to her sex. Everything inside her came to life as he took her in his mouth and made her scream his name again and again.

While there were so many unknowns in the future, what she did know was she didn't mind finding out what the future held with him at her side. Whatever became of them, she would no longer hold her breath and wait for her life to start. Going forward, she would enjoy the now, for however long it lasted.

## THE END

# ACKNOWLEDGMENTS

This series is probably the one that I held closest to my heart for so long. Even when I wanted to turn my back on the whole thing, Sara Megibow, my agent never let me forget how much I loved the story. I so appreciate your support. To my friends and family, as always, your love and encouragement serves as the wind beneath my wings.

To my besties – Amalie, MK, Sage, Shaila, and Sienna - y'all are so incredibly awesome and I don't think I would have made this writing thing work without our DMs and Girl's nights.

Thanks to my editor, Jennifer, for not allowing me to miss a beat! Rockstar status!

To all those readers, fans, and my Street Team – the Angels, I do this for you and pour a little of my soul into every word. Thank you for your continued support. I can't tell you how much I appreciate being on your e-reader/audio/bookshelf.

And to everyone I mentioned and all those I may have forgotten, remember that love is the most important thing. And I do love each of you.

Always Shine Bright
Aliza M

## ABOUT THE AUTHOR

Aliza has only ever wanted to write. Throughout her professional career in healthcare, raising two children, and eating her weight in chocolate, she never deviated from her dreams of one day, adding the notch of novelist to her belt. Author of paranormal and contemporary novels with their strong, quirky heroines in common, she continues to write the love stories of her heart. And perhaps, still eats just a little too much chocolate.

For more by Aliza Mann, visit her website at www.alizamannauthor.com.